War on a Sunday Morning

Also by Teresa R. Funke

For adults and teens:

Dancing in Combat Boots
and Other Stories of American Women
in World War II

Remember Wake

For younger readers:

The Home-Front Heroes Series

Doing My Part

The No-No Boys

V for Victory

Wave Me Good-bye

**Visit Teresa's interactive website at
www.teresafunke.com to:**

- Participate in fun Home-Front Heroes activities

- See pictures and read more about the real Home-Front Heroes

- Add your stories or your family's stories about the past

- Find out how to schedule Teresa to speak at your school or visit via webcast

War on a Sunday Morning

Teresa R. Funke

VICTORY
HOUSE
PRESS

© 2018 by Teresa R. Funke

This is a work of fiction. Names, places, and some incidents have been changed.

Published by:

Victory House Press
3836 Tradition Drive
Fort Collins, Colorado 80526
www.victoryhousepress.com

Library of Congress Control Number 2018900040

Printed in the United States of America

ISBN 978-1-935571-18-6

*To Jannie, who has kept me on course
and taught me to be bigger*

1

A New Home

December 1941

I sit cross-legged on a lawn chair facing Pearl
Harbor. It's a sunny Saturday morning, perfect for
sketching, and I have a clear view of the ships and
boats traveling up and down the Southeast Loch
past Merry Point. My gaze is focused on the USS
Oklahoma, one of the many enormous ships lined
up along Battleship Row, which I can see from
my yard. I glance down at the colored pencils in
the box in my lap and then back up at the ship,
trying to decide which pencil would best match
the medium blue color of the *Oklahoma's* hull. But
the more I study my sketch, the more I worry I'm
drawing everything wrong. The battleships aren't
big enough, for one thing. In real life they're longer
than a football field, but in my sketch they look no
larger than a tug boat. Plus, I drew a seagull over one

of the ships, and it looks as big as an airplane. And the peaks of the Waianae Mountains in the distance are much too pointed. Frustrated, I rip the page out of my sketchbook, crumple it up, and drop it on the ground.

This is what I do when I come to a new place: I draw the things that seem most important to my new home. I first started doing it when I was nine and we moved to San Diego. That was the sixth time we'd moved with the navy and the sixth house we'd lived in; somehow sketching what I saw made it, I don't know, part of me.

I'm thirteen now, and I've filled four sketchbooks. Most of the time the drawings are just for me, but this one is special. It's for Eddie Powell. He's the only one of my friends who asked me to send him sketches with my letters, and I know Eddie is fascinated by anything to do with the navy, especially the battleships. My mother is not too keen on my writing to a boy, but she knows how much I'm missing my friends so she said I can as long as I use only my initials on the outside of the envelope. That way no one can tell who sent the letter. It's more fun this way anyway – like having a secret just between Eddie and me.

The front door of our duplex swings open, and my older brother Les steps out as he pulls the drawstring closed on a large canvas bag. Les could write to any girl he wanted to, and I'm sure no one would care. Boys have it easy. He casts a look down at the ground next to my chair, and I know what he's going to do. But before I can grab it he scoops up my discarded drawing.

"Give it back," I say, leaping out of my chair and spilling my pencil box and sketchbook to the ground.

"Yep, just what I thought," he says. "Baby scribbles."

I snatch it out of his hands. "Yeah well, you couldn't draw a straight line if your life depended on it."

"Why would I want to? I have better things to do." He tightens the drawstring on the canvas bag and slings it over his shoulder.

"Where are you going?"

"None of your beeswax," he says, running his fingers through his sandy blond hair and hitching up his jeans over his skinny hips. Then he points down at my scattered pencils. "Uh oh, squirt. Don't look now, but your blue pencils are mixed up with your green ones." He laughs and trots off down the street toward the bus stop. I can tell by the clunking sound that his bag is full of ashtrays he's been making out of coconut shells. He's probably going to try to sell them to the sailors in town as cheap souvenirs. He'll have plenty of chances. There are more military men here than I've seen anywhere else. Still, Dad would be unhappy to learn Les is bothering the men with his cockamamie schemes. "That boy could find mischief in a broom closet," my mother always says, but sometimes she smiles when she says it.

So, there goes Les, off on another adventure, and here I sit as usual, drawing my "baby scribbles" and feeling sorry for myself. I should have taken Dad up on his offer to give us a tour of the base when we first moved to Hawaii three weeks ago. I could have done a close-up sketch for Eddie of Dad's ship, the USS *Oglala*, which I can't see from our house. Les went, but I said no. I was still setting up my room the way I like it, and I figured there would be plenty of other chances. But Dad says the only places he wants me to go on base are the commissary to get groceries or Bloch Arena for the dances. He says I shouldn't be "poking around" the base right now because "tensions are high," whatever that means. So, I have to draw the ships from a distance, and that's not as easy.

My father comes out the front door wearing his khaki uniform and cap, his jacket slung over his arm. I lower my feet and sit up straight. Like all navy dads, my father expects correct behavior. He scans the skies and says, "Another beautiful day, eh Rosebud?" He has said that pretty much every day since we arrived on the island.

"I guess."

He squints down at me. "Why the long face, sailor?"

"It's Esther's birthday today. She's probably having a huge party. Last year she invited our entire seventh-grade class, even the boys."

"Ah, you're missing California," he says.

"I'm missing my friends, Dad. I hate this part."

"Which part is that?"

"When we first arrive somewhere. Les settles in so quickly. All the kids think he's funny or daring, but they barely notice me. And the kids here on Oahu are so different. They whisper to each other in other languages, or say things in Pidgin English. Sometimes I know they're talking about me. And the school Mom chose is so far from the base, there aren't many navy kids there. Why do we have to be here anyway? Why can't we go back to California?"

My father squats down beside me and looks down as though he's gathering his thoughts. I know what *that* means. I'm going to get a lecture.

"Look out there, Rose," he says, waving one hand toward the harbor. "What you're looking at is the home of the United States Pacific Fleet. One mighty navy, if you ask me. These are dangerous times, kiddo, and you know why?"

Of course I know, but he's going to make me say it anyway. "Because the Nazis are trying to take over all of Europe, and the Japanese are doing the same in Asia."

"That's right. See those battleships over there? Those are our biggest and our best. There are one hundred ships in that harbor right now, and their mission is to keep us safe and make sure no one attacks *us*. I'm a part of that mission, which makes *you* a part of that mission. Do you understand?"

"Yes, sir."

"Good," Dad says, squeezing my arm gently. "Buck up, sailor. Things will get better. They always do. Don't go picking up that pidgin, though. We speak proper English in this house."

"Yes, sir."

Dad gathers up my pencils and sketchbook and hands them back to me. That's his way of helping, I guess. He always thinks staying busy solves everything, but he's put the pencils in all wrong. Some are even upside down! I straighten them out.

Dad kisses me on the head and crosses the yard in long, straight strides. At the road, he meets up with our neighbor, Mr. Barber, who gives me a wave and a loud hello. I wave back and watch them both turn the corner. Then I open the sketchbook to a clean page. Despite what Les said, I'm actually not a bad artist. At least that's what everyone tells me. Last year I won the Armistice Day poster contest at school. The principal said it was his favorite poster of all time. Eddie and Esther both say I'll have my drawings on the cover of *The Saturday Evening Post* someday. Wouldn't that be something? I pick up my black pencil and start the sketch again.

Just then, I hear the sound of music coming through the windows of the duplex next door. The front door opens and a young woman emerges. I've seen her before. She's beautiful – what Esther would call "exotic." Today she's wearing shorts and a flowery blouse tied at the waist, her wavy brown hair drawn back with a ribbon, and she's barefoot. She's carrying a bucket and has a few rags tucked under her arm.

She drops the bucket and picks up a hose to spray down her car. My brother has been admiring that car. It's a brand new Oldsmobile convertible, and it's red! She's got the top up now, of course, so the interior doesn't get wet. I flip the page and start to sketch her and her car.

After a moment she stops and looks right at me. "*Aloha*. Wanna help?"

I'm embarrassed. I didn't realize she'd seen me watching. I look down and pretend I didn't hear. But she shouts again and waves me over. "Come on. Give me a hand."

I cross the yard, and the woman offers me a wet rag. "Thanks, you're a peach," she says.

I scrub the driver's side door while she washes the back tire. "My brother loves your husband's car," I say after a minute.

"Correction: your brother loves *my* car. I bought it with my own money."

I'm shocked. Many of the women I know don't even know how to drive, much less own their own cars.

"How did you pay for it?" I ask, then bite my lip. It's rude to talk about money. But she doesn't seem to mind.

"I do some bookkeeping for my parents' store and a few other businesses."

"But you're married," I say. "Your husband doesn't mind you working?"

She puts both fists on her hips. "And what else am I supposed to do while he's off at sea for weeks? Sit around watching the grass grow?" She doesn't say it like she's angry, more like she's teasing me, and I wonder how old she is. Though she's married, she looks almost as young as me. She kind of acts that way too. I like her.

She extends a soapy hand. "I'm Leinani."

"Lei . . ."

"Leinani. It's a Hawaiian name. And you?"

"Just Rose."

"Well, Just Rose, where you from?"

"Nowhere, really. I was born in California, but we've been stationed in lots of places since then. We even lived in Panama when I was really little, but I don't remember it. The last place was Burlingame, near San Francisco."

"Well, aren't you interesting?"

"I hardly think so," I say.

"Well I do! I've never stepped foot off this island.

Who's your father?"

"Lieutenant Williams. He's a communications officer on the minelayer *Oglala*."

"A lieutenant, huh! So, why are you guys living here with us common navy folk? Why aren't you in officers' housing?"

"My mother says we're waiting for something to come available," I mutter. I'm always afraid people will think I'm all puffed up because my dad's an officer. "What does your husband do?" I ask to change the subject.

"Joe is a chief petty officer on the *Okie*. That's a battlewagon. You can see it out there, docked next to Ford Island." She points to the ship I'd been drawing earlier.

"So, why are you hanging around here on a Saturday?" she asks. "You should be swimming at the beach or going to the movies with your friends."

"Um, I don't have any friends yet. It always takes me a while. I'm kind of shy."

"You don't seem shy," she says, flicking water at me from her rag.

"Well, you're different. You're not looking at me like I'm just the new kid, and you're not calling me *haole*, whatever that means."

Leinani laughs, and it's one of those light giggles that tickles your ear. "Haole is not as bad as it sounds. It just means that you are Caucasian. People on the islands are so many things: Japanese, Chinese, Filipino, Portuguese, Hawaiian, Caucasian. No one is better than anyone else, though, so don't let it bother you. You're a *malihini*, a newcomer, so they have to tease you a bit, but don't fret, the boys will still ask you out."

As if *that* would happen. Until Eddie Powell, not a single boy has ever paid a lick of attention to me. I'm not pretty like Leinani with her huge, dark eyes. I'm just average. Average height, average weight, curly brown hair, blue eyes. And most days I'm walking around in my plaid Catholic school uniform and looking like every other girl in the class.

"Done," Leinani says. She reaches for the bucket to empty the dirty water onto the lawn. "Tell you what. Why don't we drive into town and I'll buy you an Orange Nesbitt? We can check out the beach."

"Really?"

"Of course. Get a wiggle on. We're leaving in five minutes."

As Leinani goes inside to change into a dress and "freshen up," I dash home to put away the lawn chair and carry my things inside. We're not allowed to run in the house, but I take the stairs as quickly as I can. I don't want Leinani to leave without me. I change out of my shorts into a skirt. I leave on my jersey blouse, though. The red, white, and blue colors are popular here, and the shirt looks good on me. I poke my head into my mother's bedroom. She's sitting at her sewing table, sewing a button onto my father's dress white uniform.

"Mom, can I go to town with a friend?"

"What friend?" she says, without looking up. Whenever she's doing anything for my dad, she gives it her full attention.

"Our neighbor," I say, holding my breath. Mom is usually strict about whom I pal around with.

"Have I met her?"

"Yes," I say. I mean, she probably has, right? So, it's not a lie.

"Okay, be back by suppertime."

"Thanks, Mom!"

I rush down the stairs and grab my sketchbook and pencil box on the way out. Maybe I'll be better at drawing the beach than the harbor. Leinani has pulled the car in front of my house. "Help me put the top down," she says.

I'm so excited. I've never ridden in a convertible before.

She hops in the car and ties a scarf on her head to protect her hair. I guess I should have thought of that. "Where are we going first?" I ask.

"We'll start at my parents' tourist shop. It's near Waikiki Beach."

As Leinani turns onto the highway we pick up speed. I've ridden this route before, every day on the way to St. Augustine school in Honolulu. But today, with the top down, it all feels so different. The sun warms the top of my head, the wind tosses my hair around my face, and the palm trees blur as we speed by. I can't wait to tell Les I rode in this car. For once, it will be me who had the adventure.

2

A Most Exotic Place

"What do you think of our little island? You glad to be here?" Leinani asks as she pulls up to a parking spot alongside a shop called Aloha Gifts, which is across the street from the beach.

"It's different than I thought it would be."

"How so?"

"My grandmother said Mom shouldn't bring us here. She said you all lived in grass huts and prayed to pagan gods."

Leinani laughs. "My husband thought the same thing when he arrived. He's a Brooklyn boy, and he was disappointed to see that Honolulu is just like any other American city, even though we're just a territory, not a state."

She hops out of the car, and I grab my sketchbook and follow her. There's a row of racks lined up outside her family's shop. Leinani grabs a flower *lei*. It's made of white and yellow flowers and has a tropical, almost lemony smell. "My mother makes these herself," Leinani says, draping it around my neck. "They're plumeria flowers."

"They gave us one of these when we got off the ship."

"Yes, but my mother's are the best. Now let's see how you hula." She grabs a grass skirt from another rack and wraps it quickly around my waist.

"I have no idea how!"

"It's easy, just sway your hips like this." Leinani raises her arms, elbows up and out, and takes two small steps to the right, then two steps to the left, swaying her hips as she does so. She keeps doing it, extending one arm and then the other in a wave motion.

"You're so good," I say.

"Years of hula classes. My mother made me take them."

A woman appears in the doorway, and Leinani introduces her as her mother, Mrs. Kamaka.

"*E komo mai,*" Mrs. Kamaka says to me, which I'm told means, "Welcome. Come in." Mrs. Kamaka is shorter than Leinani, but just as beautiful. She tells us Leinani's father has gone to the bank.

Inside, Leinani shows me more souvenirs: nose

flutes, wooden bowls, and handmade silk aloha shirts with palm tree patterns. "None of those cheap touristy items in this shop. My parents buy the good stuff," she says. I think of my brother and his lousy ashtrays and smirk. She hands me a book on Hawaiian folklore and legends. "Here, these stories are like nothing you'll read in school. This is real adventure. Kauhuhu, the shark god, Pele the goddess of volcanoes, love stories that will break your heart. Don't tell your grandparents, though."

I glance at the illustrations in the book and wonder if Eddie would find these stories interesting.

We turn and see a young Oriental girl emerging from a back room holding a broom. Leinani skips over and locks arms with her.

"Rose, this is June Nakamura."

"I know," I say. "We're in the same class at school." June helped me find my classroom on the first day I arrived and she's talked to me a few times, but mostly she hangs out with her best friend Myrna. Every day after school they leave at a run. I wonder where they go.

"I know June from long time," Leinani says in that local pidgin they all seem to know. "She good egg." She gives June a playful nudge then switches back to standard English for my sake. "June and her mother help around the shop. Her father is a fisherman on a *sampan* boat."

"Not anymore," June says, grinning broadly. "He's a captain now."

"That's wonderful, June! When did that happen?"

"Last week. He finally saved up enough to buy his own boat."

"What's a sampan?" I ask.

"It's a Japanese fishing boat," June says. "They fish at Kewalo Basin, mostly for *ahi* and *aku*."

I have no idea what that means.

"Ahi is a kind of tuna," Leinani explains, seeing my confusion. "This girl has a lot to learn, June. I'm taking her over to the beach. I'll ask my mother if you can take a break and join us." Leinani tells us to wait here for a minute. June and I stand in awkward silence.

"Did you get your homework done?" I finally ask.

"Not yet. I've been here all morning."

"Of course," I say. And we both look at our shoes.

"Come on, you two. We're wasting daylight," Leinani says. We pop into a corner store nearby, and Leinani buys us each an Orange Nesbitt soda. I hold the icy bottle to my cheek. The temperature must be close to 80 degrees, which still seems strange to me for the first weekend in December. And the humidity is only a little sticky on the skin. My grandmother had said it would feel like you'd just stepped out of a hot bath, but it's really not bad. Besides, the island breezes keep you cool.

Leinani leads us down a walkway that opens onto a beautiful, sandy beach. I shade my eyes, but I still can't see the end of the beach. It must go on for miles. There are thousands of people here, much more than used to gather at the cold-water beaches back in Burlingame. Some people lounge on chairs under umbrellas, but most sit or lie in the warm sand or on blankets or mats. Most of the people wear bathing suits, but there are also lots of soldiers and sailors in uniforms escorting girls in bright, summery dresses.

The turquoise ocean lies before us. To the east a saucer-shaped hill juts toward the sea. "That's Diamond Head," Leinani says. "It's the cone of a volcano. The Hawaiians named it Le'ahi because they thought the shape of the crater looked like the dorsal fin on the back of a tuna."

Leinani kicks off her shoes and leads us to the perfect spot on the beach to see the surfers. The water is full of them, mostly boys or young men wearing red or blue bathing trunks, their bare chests glittering in the sun. On a couple of boards, though, girls ride along. On only one board do I see a girl by herself.

Watching the surfers is like watching a ballet. They lie on their surfboards and wait for just the right moment to catch a wave. Then they rise side by side, skimming along much faster than I would have imagined. They stand toward the back of their boards, the front ends lifting slightly out of the water. One boy does a headstand on his board, another lifts a girl onto his shoulders. She holds her arms out straight for balance. "Look at that," I say.

"Uh oh." Leinani points to a surfer who has pitched sideways off his board and hit the water hard. "That's called a wipeout. What you say, Rose? You surf?" Leinani asks.

"No! It looks kinda scary."

"Nah, it's easy," Leinani jumps to her feet and pretends to balance on a board before standing up straight and leaning back slightly, as if she owns the imaginary water beneath her. "Just relax and let the waves take you."

I've never met a girl with so much confidence, and just being around her makes me feel more confident too.

"How old are you, Leinani?"

"I'm twenty. And don't tell me I look younger, I already know. You girls stay here. I gotta say hi to the lifeguard. He's a friend of mine." She runs across the beach, kicking up sand as she goes.

"She's great, isn't she?" June says.

"I've never met anyone like her. Hey, June, can I ask you something?"

"Sure."

"I've seen you and Myrna rushing somewhere after school. Where do you go?"

"Japanese school, and the teacher hates it when we're late."

"What's Japanese school?"

"Nothing special. We just learn about the language and the customs of Japan."

"Were you born there?"

"No, I was born right here in Honolulu," she says emphatically. "But my parents are from Japan, and they want us kids to keep up the culture. Lots of Japanese kids in Hawaii go. It's not that unusual."

I hope I didn't say the wrong thing. It's so hard to be someplace new when everyone thinks you should know things you don't. That's why I mostly keep to myself for a while when we get to a different place, to figure things out so I don't put my foot in my mouth.

"Is that a sketchbook?" June asks. She doesn't seem annoyed so I guess I'm okay.

"Yes. Do you draw?"

"A little," she says. "Mostly dogs."

"I love dogs!"

"Me too, but I've never been allowed to have one."

"We had one when I was very little, but I don't remember it," I say.

"Did it die?"

"No, we had to leave it behind when we moved to Panama. My mom says I cried so much that she vowed never to own another dog. She says it's not practical with all our moves."

"That's sad. My mother just says dogs are not clean. That's it," June says. "Can I see your sketchbook?"

"Um, I guess, but I'm not very good."

"That's okay," June says.

Reluctantly, I hand over the book.

As she flips through the drawings I explain them. "That's the Matson liner we sailed over on, and those are the Hawaiian girls who met our ship to welcome us with leis. That's our duplex. Those are just some songbirds I've seen in the yard. Oh, and that's a friend of mine, Eddie."

"Your boyfriend?" June nudges me.

"Not exactly. Mostly just a friend."

"Too bad. He's a dreamboat."

"Oh, he's actually better looking than this. I got the hair right and I'm getting better at eyes, but I'm still having trouble with noses."

"Noses are hard. And hands. Those are the hardest," June says. "Mr. Takahashi, my teacher at Japanese school, is really good. He's been helping me. So, what are you going to sketch now?"

"I don't know, the surfers maybe. What do you think I should draw?"

June looks around, then turns to me with a sly grin. "How 'bout him? Would Eddie mind?" she says, pointing to a handsome Hawaiian boy. We both giggle.

And then I see something that gets my full attention. Not fifty feet away is my brother, Les, walking bold as brass alongside a sailor and his girl, showing them one of his ashtrays. The sailor pushes him roughly out of the way, and my brother kicks sand at him. The sailor turns unexpectedly and grabs a fistful of my brother's shirt. Les drops his bag and raises his hands in a show of surrender. I jump to my feet, wondering if I should try to help, but the sailor's girlfriend tugs on his arm. He shoves my brother backward. Les trips over his bag and falls flat on his rump. The sailor laughs and turns to walk away with his girl.

"Come on," I say to June. "That's my brother." As we approach, Les stands and dusts the sand off his jeans. He seems mildly surprised to see me.

"Who's your friend?" he asks. If he's upset about his encounter with the sailor it doesn't show. Les is always in trouble with someone. I guess he's used to it.

"This is June. She's in my class."

"Wanna see what I made?" Les grins, tugging at the drawstring to open his sack.

I grab his hands to stop him. "No, she does not want to see your crummy ashtrays."

"Suit yourself," Les says. He takes a few dollar bills out of his pocket. "Not a bad day's work, eh? Hey, June, come to the dance tonight at Bloch Arena and I'll buy you a soda." He winks at her.

"Let's go," I say, before she can answer. I make it a point not to let my brother anywhere near my friends. And though June and I are not friends yet, we might be.

"For the record, I wouldn't dance with my brother ever, unless you want black and blue toes. He's a real dead hoofer."

"Who's a dead hoofer?" Leinani asks, coming up beside us. We tell her about my brother and the dance. "Oh yes, you should come, June! They're having the 'Battle of Music' competition tonight between the ship bands. Everyone will be there. The navy bands are real smooth."

"Can I stay the night at your place again?" June asks. "My parents don't like me taking the bus home late."

"Of course! We'll have so much fun," Leinani says. "Rose can come with us." Before I can answer, she points at my empty soda bottle. "You *pau*?"

I assume that means "done" in Hawaiian or maybe pidgin or both, so I hand her the bottle. "See," Leinani says, draping her arm around my shoulder, "you catch on fast. We're gonna have you feeling at home here in no time. June and I need to get back to the store, but you can stay here and sketch if you want. I'll come get you when I'm done going over the accounts with my mother."

"Hey, Rose," June says. "Bring your sketchbook to school on Monday, and you can come with me to Japanese school. You can show your sketches to Mr. Takahashi."

"Oh, I don't know."

"Come on! It'll be okay. Mr. Takahashi is really nice."

I nod and hug my sketchbook to my chest. As they walk away I sit down in the sand, arranging my skirt just so beneath me. I open the sketchbook to a new page and start a picture of the beach and the surfers. If Eddie could see me now!

3

Battle of Music

When Leinani, Joe, and June knock on the door after supper, I recognize Joe immediately. I've seen him walking by the house. He's pretty swoony with his broad shoulders and rich brown eyes. I invite them in to chat with my parents. Joe is very formal around my father, but when we leave my parents' house and cross the street to Bloch Arena, he changes. He has us all laughing as he tells a story about a dance he went to as a kid back in Brooklyn. He says he borrowed some trousers from his older brother, but they were too big. While he was dancing with this girl he really liked they slipped off. Leinani laughs the hardest and kisses him on the cheek as they walk arm in arm.

Bloch Arena is packed with people, mostly soldiers and sailors and lots of the wives and families. They sit on the wooden bleachers and mingle on the gym floor as the bands set up. Everyone has come out to see the semifinals between the ships' musicians. Leinani says the *Arizona* band is the best, but they're not playing tonight. Bands from the *Pennsylvania*, the *Tennessee*, and the *Argonne* will compete. Our neighbors Mr. and Mrs. Barber stop to say hello.

"Good evening, pretty lady," Mr. Barber says to me. "Did you come to break some hearts?"

I blush, and Mrs. Barber tells her husband not to tease me. I introduce June, and Mrs. Barber asks us about school and if we're excited about Christmas. I tell her I am, though it will be strange to be someplace so sunny and warm on Christmas Day.

Then the *Pennsylvania* band begins to play, and the Barbers leave to find seats higher up in the bleachers. Joe and Leinani offer to get us all sodas. After they leave, it's just June and me. As I get to know her better, I realize she's not only nice, she's really funny. Not quite as funny as Esther, but pretty close. She starts this game where she chooses someone in the crowd and imagines what they might be saying. She points to a sailor who is talking to two teenage boys and imagines him trying to recruit them for the military. He says to one, "Uncle Sam wants you." And then to the other, "But maybe not you. You're a little scrawny." She points to an older woman with a hat that looks like a bird's nest and has her say, "Has anyone seen my parakeet?" And then she spots my brother trying to impress some girl who's looking at him like he's from Mars. June imagines him saying, "Hey, can I give you a ride home? My spaceship is right outside" and "Your eyes are as pretty as the valleys of Jupiter." I laugh so hard I snort, which makes us both laugh even more.

Joe and Leinani return and ask what's so funny, but we keep it to ourselves. It would probably sound silly to them, but it sure was funny to us.

Two of Joe's shipmates, Ted and Larry, come over to join us. Ted is blond and stocky and has a Southern accent. He asks if we like card tricks and then pulls out a deck to show June and me a new trick he's learned. Larry is tall, beanpole thin, and from St. Louis. He was recently stationed in Burlingame too! We talk about California, and he shows us pictures of his fiancée, who is still there. Joe invites me to dance. I refuse at first, but Joe won't take no for an answer. He leads me out to the dance floor, and I'm glad I started practicing in my room lately. I only step on his feet a couple of times, but he just laughs. He dances with June after me, and she's much better than I am.

When they announce the jitterbug contest, Joe and Leinani enter. Just before the music begins, the announcer brings up a ten-year-old girl and says he happens to know she's a good dancer. He asks if anyone would like to be her partner. Ted is about to volunteer, but some other sailor beats him to it.

"Can you imagine having the guts to do something like that when you were only ten?" I say to June. "I never would have."

"Yeah, that kid's a real go-getter."

The band kicks up a roof-raising version of "Jingle Bells." Ted suggests we stand on the bleacher to see better. He gives us a hand up as the dancers start to move. They step to the side, then rock back; slow, slow, quick, quick. Ted jumps up beside me and tries to get me to sway in time to the music. I'm embarrassed, but I do it. And it's kind of fun. Larry cups his hands around his mouth and shouts, "Go get 'em, Joey!"

Then all the dancers start doing their own versions of turns, dips, and swing-outs. Joe and Leinani look great, except she keeps laughing and throwing Joe off, and he has to pull her in tight to get her back on track. In the end, though, it's the little girl, Patsy, and her partner who win. The crowd goes wild. She and the sailor even get trophies!

"No fair," June says. "I'd like a trophy."

"We should practice together before the next dance," I say.

"Great idea!"

At the end of the night, the *Pennsylvania* band is declared the winner. Some people boo, others cheer, and Joe teases a friend who is from the *Argonne*, telling him his ship never had a chance.

As the midnight curfew approaches, hundreds of people slowly stream out of the arena talking and laughing. Just outside a fight breaks out between two servicemen, but that happens all the time, so we just walk right past. I notice, though, that my brother is watching the fight. Typical!

Ted and Larry have to get back to the *Oklahoma* that night. They're on duty. But Leinani, Joe, June, and I wander down to the water to chat about the evening. In the moonlight, we can see the silhouette of a nearby boat and hear the waves gently lapping at the shore. Some lone trumpet player sounds a few notes on his instrument as he heads back to base. Joe tells us how he grew up admiring the big ships in New York Harbor and how he always wanted to sail the seas.

June talks about how her father sometimes takes them out on his sampan in the evenings and cooks them pancakes for supper. He lets her steer with the rod at the end of the boat. She says maybe I can come with them sometime.

I tell them how Dad used to invite us to come aboard his ship back in California and have dinner with him and the other officers and then watch a movie with all the men. And how he had to remind Les every time not to run on deck.

As we stand up to head home, I hear my name and see my brother waving me over. I ask the others to wait a minute and go to join him. He's standing with a Chinese boy who looks a little younger than me.

"Rose, this here's Jimmy Hu," Les says. "His cousin is dating a fella on the *Pennsylvania*. I was just tellin' Jimmy how I caught that rattlesnake back in Idaho with my bare hands. He don't believe me. Tell him."

As I recall, the snake was barely moving. I think it was almost dead. But I don't want to embarrass my brother in front of his new friend. "That's right, he did. Picked it right up by the tail."

"See, told ya."

"You one crazy haole," Jimmy says in that Pidgin English my father hates. "I going find my cousin. Don't forget da moolah you owe me."

"Yeah, yeah," Les says, and I wonder what that's all about, but Les won't tell me. He falls in step with the rest of us, though, and we walk back to navy housing. In my room that night, I realize I'm exhausted but happy, really happy, for the first time since we moved here. Even though it's late, I start a letter to Esther to tell her about the dance and the contest. Tomorrow I'll finish my sketches of the harbor and the beach for Eddie. If I get them in the mail soon, they should reach him before Christmas. I guess Dad was right. Things are starting to look up.

4

An Unexpected Attack

The next day, I wake to the sound of hammering. My father is fixing something. Never mind that it's 7:00 a.m. on a Sunday morning. I groan and drag my pillow over my head, but I can still hear it. Might as well get up.

I make my bed first and straighten one of my movie star pictures above the headboard. I always keep them in the same order: Ronald Reagan and Frank Sinatra on top, Veronica Lake and Linda Darnel on the bottom. Then I open my closet door, and hanging right at the front is my favorite rose-colored dress. I always move the outfit I'm going to wear the next day to the front of the closet before I go to bed each night. Dad says if I wasn't a girl, I'd make a great sailor because the navy is all about schedules and keeping things just so.

I hear a commotion outside my open window and go to look. Les is getting on his bike, and I wonder where he's going so early. Les would *not* make a good sailor. There is nothing predictable about my brother. Well, wherever he's going, he'd better be back in time for church or he'll have Dad *and* Mom to answer to.

I take out the rag curlers I slept in, brush out my hair, and pull the sides back with bobby pins. I write three pages of my letter to Esther, and then my stomach growls. I grab my saddle shoes and carry them and my sketchbook downstairs. I ask Mom if I can turn on the radio, and she says yes if I set the formal table in the front room. Dad has gone upstairs to shave and calls down for me to turn up the music.

"Breakfast is almost ready," Mom says. "Go outside and see if you can spot your brother."

I reach for my shoes, and then decide to step barefoot onto the lawn.

I scan the street from left to right, but there is no sign of Les. There is, though, the distinct rumble of planes approaching. That's nothing unusual. Hickam airfield is right next door to our housing unit, and planes are often in the air above our house. It's a little odd, though, for our pilots to be practicing maneuvers so early on a Sunday morning. I shield my eyes with my hand as the first planes pass over with a low roar. They are headed for the harbor and flying so low I can see the head of the pilot, his goggles up on his forehead. Instinctively I wave, but he does not wave back. And then I notice a white scarf around his neck, and as the plane passes, I observe something else. There are red painted balls on the undersides of his wings. And slowly it dawns on me . . . those are not red balls. They are the Rising Sun. The insignia of Japan. These are enemy planes!

Then from all around I hear deafening explosions and what sounds like firecrackers going off, and then the rattle of machine gun fire. And now it seems like the planes are everywhere, coming from all directions, and there are black things falling from their underbellies as they cross over the harbor in front of me and over the airfield to my left. There's an explosion in the harbor, and then another, and another. Huge spouts of water spray up around the ships. Bombs are falling! *Boom, boom, boom!!* I plug my ears. Dad said there were one hundred ships in the harbor. Given all the noise and commotion, it seems to me the Japanese are trying to sink every one.

Dark plumes of smoke start to rise from Battleship Row. The planes are hitting those big battlewagons with all they've got. Joe's ship, the *Oklahoma*, has been struck. The whole ship jumps in the air. I know Joe's not on board, but Ted and Larry are. A fist grips my heart. I squeeze my eyes closed then open them slowly. At the same time I remove my fingers from my ears, hoping that somehow what I'm seeing and hearing will go back to normal. But it doesn't. Then the smell comes toward me, oil burning, and it's almost as if I can taste it. And then, not three feet from where I'm standing, a large piece of metal shrapnel hits the ground. This jolts me to my senses.

I stumble backward toward the house and yank open the screen door. "Daddy, hurry. It's the Japanese." A few moments later, my father joins me on the porch. He's changed into his uniform pants and shirt, and there is still a bit of shaving cream below his ear. My mother is standing in the front doorway, as if she's frozen to the spot. All she says is, "Les."

I follow my dad onto the lawn. "It's starting, Rose," he says.

And then it becomes clear to me: This is the attack Dad always said would never happen, despite all the rumors. These are the pilots Les said would be too afraid to take on America. This is the reason Mom's been stockpiling cans of food and even Hershey's bars and saying, "It's just good to be prepared." This is what Dad and Mom have been talking about all those times they'd grow quiet the minute Les or I entered the room. This is the war I've only heard mentioned in whispers.

Joe and Leinani come out of their house, she in her nightgown and floral robe, and he in his trousers, shoes, and undershirt. He's holding his uniform shirt and looking at his ship. He's pressing his palms against his head, like he's trying to push the picture from his mind. Through the smoke, we can see a huge waterspout erupt near the *Oklahoma*, and then the ship lists to the side.

"She's gonna roll over!" Joe says.

It's like we're watching all the big ships die. The Japanese planes are strafing the bows of the ships' decks with bullets, trying to hit as many sailors as they can. And now the sky is also filled with black and white bursts of smoke from our own anti-aircraft fire, as our men take aim at the enemy planes.

My father grabs me by the shoulders. "Go inside, Rose. You and your mother hide under the table. Don't come out until it's over. When your brother gets home, tell him to *stay put.*"

"Where are you going?"

"To the base."

"I'll go with you," Joe says to Dad.

Leinani reaches for Joe and tries to hold him back. He turns to kiss her and says something, then pulls away and runs to join my father, buttoning his shirt as he goes. Only then do I notice June standing off to the side, her hand over her mouth, her eyes wide. I'd forgotten she had stayed the night at Leinani's.

I should go inside like my father told me, but I wait until I see Joe and him turn the corner headed for the main gate of the base. Just then, another plane flies directly over our duplex and starts strafing the cars parked in the little lot across from our house. The cars bounce as the bullets hit, and the ground beneath our feet starts to shake. Leinani pushes June back inside her duplex, and Mom and I rush back into our house.

"Dad wants us under the table," I say. "Come on."

"It's not enough protection," Mom says. "We need a mattress." We run upstairs and rip the mattress off my bed. As we're bumping it down the stairs, we hear something hit the roof. We pause and glance up, wondering if the roof is going to collapse or maybe catch on fire. When nothing happens, we hurry down the stairs and throw the mattress on top of the table.

We stay under the table for another thirty minutes or so. The radio is still on, but the music has stopped. We hear the announcer say, *All military personnel are under orders to return to their stations immediately,* and I think about my father and wonder if he's on board his ship or if his ship is even still above water.

My mother pulls out her rosary beads and nudges me to pray along. I close my eyes and pray as hard as I can. Only when we can't hear the planes overhead anymore do we venture out to take a peek. I look first out the window, and then Mom eases the front door open. We take one timid step outside. The air is filled with smoke, and explosions are still coming from the ships, but it seems mostly clear near our house. Out in the harbor, though, Joe's ship has "turned turtle" as my brother would say. It's almost completely upside down. I can no longer see Ford Island behind her. It is hidden by huge, billowy clouds of black, black smoke.

Leinani and June come to stand beside us.

They're looking at the *Oklahoma* too, tears in their eyes.

"I'm sure Joe is fine," I say to Leinani, though my voice doesn't sound as confident as my words. "He wasn't on the ship," I remind us both.

"No, but he could've been. It was just good luck he was off duty. But what about the others?"

She means Larry and Ted and the rest, of course. Did they get off the ship in time? Or were they trapped inside when she sank?

"Look!" I say. Our neighbor, Mrs. Barber, is limping along the road, blood running her leg. "Mrs. Barber is hurt."

We run to help her.

"It's nothing," Mrs. Barber says. "Just some shrapnel from the shells. It's falling everywhere." I turn to see if that's what hit our roof, a big piece of shrapnel, or maybe an unexploded shell. Instead, I see a dead duck, its wing hanging over the eaves. It must have been knocked from the air.

"Let me help you," Mom says.

But Mrs. Barber shakes her head. "I'm fine. I got the shrapnel out. It's just bleeding a little now. I need to get home to my husband. He was still in bed when I left. I just went out for my morning walk and then

. . . this." Mrs. Barber reaches for my mother's hands. "You ladies stay inside and stick together. Gather what you can to protect yourselves. I'm sure the Japanese will invade soon. Who knows, they might already be in the city. I need to go." We watch her hobble off down the street.

June grabs Leinani's arm. "Do you think it's true? Are they bombing the city? My parents are there."

"Yes, I should get you home," Leinani says. "I'll get my car."

"I'll go with you," I offer. "We can look for my brother on the way."

"Where is Les?"

"We don't know," Mom says. "He left this morning, and he's not back yet."

But before we can think about doing anything more, we hear them. *Planes!* They're coming back. I grab Leinani and June and drag them toward my house. "Mrs. Barber said we should stick together," I insist.

The ground shakes again with this new attack, and it's like running with rubber legs. I scream as I trip and fall, but Mom pulls me quickly to my feet.

Inside, we crawl back under the table. It's a tight fit with four of us. We hear the radio announcer,

Webley Edwards, telling the folks in the city what we already know. *All right now, listen carefully. The island of Oahu is being attacked by enemy planes. The center of this attack is Pearl Harbor, but the planes are attacking airfields as well. We are under attack. There seems to be no doubt about it. Do not go out on the streets. Keep under cover and keep calm. Some of you may think that this is just another military maneuver. This is not a maneuver. This is the real McCoy!*

I wriggle out from under the table.

Mom grabs at my dress. "Where are you going?"

"I need to get my sketchbook."

"Rose, no," she says, but I twist out of her grip and dash up to my room, only to remember I took it down to the kitchen this morning. I run back downstairs just as another huge explosion rocks the harbor. I snatch my sketchbook off the kitchen table and return to the front room. Mom and Leinani pull me back under the table. I open to an empty page and start to sketch frantically, my hand never lifting from the paper. Oddly, I'm sketching the same scene I was working on yesterday, only now the sky is not blue, it's black. And the ships are not lined up peacefully, they are pell-mell and burning, and there are no seagulls in the air, only Japanese dive bombers. A tear hits the paper, and I realize I'm crying.

"It's okay," Mom says. "Keep going. You're doing well."

And it's suddenly more important than ever that I get this sketch right. People need to know what happened here. They need to see it. I draw everything I could see from our front yard: the corner of Bloch Arena, the yellow navy headquarters building, the big hammerhead crane in the dockyard, even the cars parked in the lot across from our house, the ones that now have bullet holes in their hoods.

I stop only when an eerie silence sets in around 10:00 a.m. None of us move, though, for another twenty minutes, waiting to be sure the attack is really over and wondering if the Japanese soldiers have already landed on the island.

"Mrs. Williams," Leinani says. "What do you have for protection? Do you have a gun?"

My mother shakes her head. "We'll just have to find other things," she says. "Ladies, gather anything you can think of and put it on the kitchen table."

My mother and June go to the kitchen and bring back cooking knives and a pair of scissors. Leinani and I scour the closets and cupboards. We find a hammer and a large flashlight.

"Is that it?" I ask, wondering how two women and two thirteen-year-old girls are supposed to defend themselves with such silly weapons.

"Wait," Mom says. She rummages in a drawer and pulls out a rolling pin. She sets it on the table alongside the knives. It looks so ridiculous we all start to laugh. All except Mom. She thinks we're laughing at her, but we're not. We're laughing because we can't help it. And then she starts laughing too. We stop abruptly, though, when we hear a knock on the door.

My mother puts her finger to her lips and crosses the front room. She asks through the closed door who it is. Our next-door neighbor, Mrs. Lowe, announces herself, and Mom opens the door. There stands Mrs. Lowe, holding her twin baby girls, Susie and Sharon. Her husband is assigned to the *Arizona*, which, like my father's ship and Joe's, is docked in the harbor. And like those ships, it's been getting hammered. She asks if she can come in. We let her, of course. She tells us she's been holding the babies since the attack first started more than two hours ago, afraid to put them down in case she needed to run. She looks exhausted. She's wearing a house dress and her hair is still in curlers.

June and I step forward to take her babies. She hands Susie to me and is about to hand over Sharon when she seems to get a good look at June.

"Are you a *Jap*?" she asks, and I gasp. I mean, people say that word all the time, even though they shouldn't, but I've never heard it said so rudely to someone's face. "What are you *doing* here?" Mrs. Lowe demands.

"She's with me," Leinani says. "It's okay. She's a friend." Leinani reaches for Sharon, and Mrs. Lowe slowly lets go of the baby.

As Mom shows our neighbor to the washroom, Leinani tries to hand Sharon to June, but June won't take her. She crosses her arms tightly, hunches her shoulders, and backs up against the wall. Leinani and I sit down on the davenport, and I hug Susie to me. She puts her tiny fists against my chest and pushes me back. When I ease up, she gives me a long look, like she's sizing me up, then pops her thumb in her mouth. She's so cute, I can't help but smile. I smooth the dark curls on Susie's head and sigh.

"What do we do now?" I ask Leinani.

"I guess we wait."

5

You Must Evacuate

At 11:41 we are gathered around the radio, as we
have been all morning. Governor Poindexter is
declaring a "state of emergency." I'm not sure exactly
what that means, but the adults don't seem interested
in explaining it. In fact, they don't seem interested in
talking much at all anymore. Shortly after that, the
radio stations are ordered off the air, and that makes
us feel even more alone.

Leinani and June try to call their parents, but the
phone operator tells them to keep the lines open.
They decide to head to town, and I convince Mom
to let me ride along as far as the highway to look for
Les. When we reach the highway, though, it is one
big traffic jam. Soldiers and sailors are coming from
town trying to get back to base, and truckloads and
carloads of wounded men are heading the other
direction toward the hospitals in town. We get out of
Leinani's car and stand beside it, watching the trucks

with the wounded pass. One man is leaning against the truck rails, clearly unconscious. Another is badly burned, his singed clothes barely clinging to his body. Another is covered in oil.

My gaze locks on one young man who looks familiar, and I recognize him. It's Larry from the dance. I raise my hand to wave, but he's staring past me. His eyes are dull and his skin is pale. He's wearing no shirt, and I can see tracks of dirt and blood on his chest. There's a bloody bandage wrapped around his chest and another around his stomach. And all I can think about is that picture he showed me of his fiancée and how happy he seemed last night. And then the truck moves on. A military police officer tells us to quit blocking the road, and we turn around and head home.

We sit in silence for a while, each lost in our own thoughts. Then Mom says we should eat something, and I help her put together some sandwiches. We sit at the small kitchen table, but none of us have much of an appetite. Mrs. Lowe and Mom pull out the davenport, where Les sleeps each night, to make a bed. We lay the babies in the middle for a nap. Mrs. Lowe lies down with them. She says it's to help them sleep, but I'm not sure that's the only reason. She doesn't seem well.

"Sick with worry," Mom whispers to me when I point out how she looks. I know the feeling. We've heard nothing from my father yet, or Joe, or Les, and every now and then one of us goes to the window just hoping. The skies over the harbor and the airfield are still full of smoke, the fires are burning, and we still hear anti-aircraft fire from time to time, though we can't imagine what our guys are shooting at now.

Soon, an MP arrives. He tells us the navy is going to evacuate us to town. We should grab only what we absolutely need, he says. He'll wait. Leinani and June scurry off to gather their things.

"We can't go," Mom tells the MP. "My son hasn't come home yet!"

"How old is he?"

"Fifteen."

"Old enough to fend for himself," the MP says. "I'm sure he's fine. We need to clear this area, ma'am. I need you to cooperate *now*."

My mother knows better than to defy a military order. She shoots me a dismayed look, but tells me to grab her handbag and a couple of blankets while she writes a note to my brother and father. My hands are shaking as I collect our things. I'm not sure how long we'll be gone, or if we'll be coming back. I grab a couple of blankets, plus light sweaters for me, my mother, and even Les. No one really seems to need sweaters in Hawaii, even in the dead of winter, but you never know. I slip on the pink seashell bracelet Eddie gave me. I haven't worn it up till now. I've been hiding it under my pillow to keep Les from finding out. He would've teased me unmercifully. Now I'd welcome his teasing if I just knew he was okay. Mom calls for me to hurry, and I look around for my sketchbook but remember it's still on the coffee table in the living room.

When I go back downstairs, Mrs. Lowe is still sitting on the davenport. "My babies," she says, her eyes pleading.

"Rose, go with her," Mom says. "We'll watch the babies."

I give Mom our stuff and follow Mrs. Lowe to her duplex. We collect as many diapers, clothes, and bottles as time will allow. Mom carries our belongings and some of Mrs. Lowe's things, and Mrs. Lowe and I each carry a baby. With Leinani and June, we head for the school bus that is waiting. As other women emerge from their homes, they are toting the strangest things. One holds a fur coat, another a parrot in a cage, another a ceramic teapot. Their children step lively, trying to keep up.

Mom and I board the bus and sit across the aisle from Leinani and June. I'm still holding Susie. Mrs. Lowe sits behind me cradling Sharon. Mrs. Barber boards the bus, her leg all bandaged up. She squeezes my shoulder gently as she passes us looking for a seat.

"Did they say where we are going?" I ask June.

"Leinani asked, but the guard wouldn't tell us. Somewhere safe is all he'd say."

"Someone said the Army-Navy YMCA on Hotel Street," the woman in front of us whispers.

"I hope that's true," June says to me. "I can maybe sneak off there and walk home. I have to make sure my parents are safe." The baby reaches over and plucks at June's blouse, but June scoots closer to Leinani and turns her head away.

It's slow going to reach town. The highway is still packed with vehicles. The bus driver gets off the main road as soon as he can and starts weaving through back streets. Everyone on the bus is quiet, even the kids. We are looking for signs of destruction, or maybe for Japanese troops. I see a car pass by with huge bullet holes in its side. And there's a building with the windows blown out and the roof partly off, and another that is smoldering, as if a fire were just put out. We pass several buildings with pock marks in the walls from shrapnel and bullets, and in some yards we see spent shells from our big guns, broken tree limbs, and other bits of wreckage. The damage is not the same everywhere, though. It seems to have come down to luck as to who got hit and who didn't. Someone says she heard a bomb landed in front of the governor's mansion. Another says she heard a radio reporter on KTU radio station say a bomb dropped within 50 feet of the radio tower. Leinani groans. I know she's thinking about her parents and hoping their shop was not hit.

Finally, we pull up to the YMCA and unload. It's a beautiful building surrounded by palm trees and flowers, much prettier than any Y I've ever seen. As we're walking up the double staircase, Leinani tells me she met Joe here. He approached her after a hula program and asked if she'd like to see a movie that night. Her mother, who always came with her, did not want her to go. Her parents didn't trust the military men, but Leinani said she had a good feeling about Joe so her mother invited him to dinner instead.

"We haven't even been married a year," she says, her voice cracking.

We are directed toward the gym. It is filling fast with military families. The lady behind me says to the attendant, "This building isn't big enough for all of us."

"Of course it is," he says. "We had five hundred servicemen here last night. Saturday nights are always busy. We'll find everyone a place."

The corners of the room have already been taken so we head toward the center, and I spread out the blankets carefully. Immediately the nearby women turn to talk to us. They ask what we've heard, and they tell us the rumors. One woman says the Japanese plantation farmers had cut arrows in the cane fields to direct the enemy planes. Another says she heard Japanese parachutists had already landed somewhere on Oahu. Another says she heard our water might be poisoned.

"They'll be landing on the beaches soon," one woman says matter-of-factly. Instantly I imagine huge Japanese warships surrounding the island and beautiful Waikiki Beach swarming with Japanese soldiers, rifles and bayonets pointed toward town. For all we know, their planes and submarines may have already returned to the base, destroying what's left of our planes and ships. And my father might be right in the middle of all that. Les too.

"I need to go," June says to me.

"Are you sure?"

"My house isn't far. I'll be fine."

"I'll walk you out," I say. But as we reach the stairs, I see a guard standing there, and June and I exchange a look. What if he won't let her go?

"Don't worry," I say, my heart beating a little faster. "I have an idea." I slip the bracelet off my wrist and into my pocket and tell June to hang back.

"Can you help me?" I say, approaching the guard. "I lost my bracelet and it means the world to me. My father gave it to me, and now he's out there fighting, and I just *have* to find it. I think I dropped it when we came in."

The guard looks around his feet, and I motion to June to step behind him as I drop to my hands and knees. She looks at me with surprise and mouths the words "thank you" as she leaves. When the guard is looking the other way, I sneak the bracelet from my pocket. "I found it," I say. "Thanks ever so much."

Feeling proud of myself, I return to the gym, and Leinani asks where I went. I tell her.

"I should go too," Leinani says. "Check on my parents. But what if they make an announcement? What if there's news about Joe?"

The Lowe babies start to cry. They aren't the only ones. The gym is filled with the sounds of wailing babies, whining children, and scolding mothers. It's too crowded to let the children play, and everyone's nerves are on edge. I take out my sketchbook and start to record the scene. A little boy about four years old wanders over and picks up my pencil box. "Would you like to draw?" I ask him. He nods and plunks down beside me. I tear out a piece of paper, and he grabs a black pencil and starts making frantic spirals on the page. Then he adds blue lines below it, and I realize he's drawing what he saw in the harbor this morning, just like I did. He's pressing so hard the paper starts to tear.

I pat him on the back and turn to scan the room. I wonder how I'm ever going to draw all these faces, all these women and children scared to death, wishing somehow this was all just a bad dream. But I decide to try.

About an hour later, I look up from my sketch and see a familiar figure in the doorway. It takes me a minute to believe it's really him, my dad! My usually polished father is covered with dirt and oil and maybe blood. His shoes are scuffed and his hands are scratched. He points at me and then my mother, who has just seen him too. We both pick our way through the crowd to reach him. He tries to usher us into the hallway, but we are too busy hugging him and pummeling him with questions.

He tells us quickly that by the time he reached the *Oglala*, it was too late to do anything. In short order, she rolled over. "I don't think she took a direct hit. The poor old girl probably died of fright," he says with a strained chuckle. I'm sure he thinks by being funny he'll lessen our concerns, but it's not going to work.

"What about the men?" my mother asks.

"Fine. They got off the ship in time."

"What did you do then?" I ask.

"I ran to the hospital to see if I could help."

When Mrs. Lowe hears that, she approaches my father. So do some of the other women.

"My husband was on the *Nevada*," one lady says. "They say she was hit bad but she's still afloat. He's Ensign Holder, do you know him?"

"My man was on the *Oklahoma*."

"Mine was on the *California*. Gordon Summers."

"What about Emmett?" Mrs. Lowe asks. "They're saying the *Arizona* has been sunk, but some of the men made it off. Is that true, Lieutenant Williams?"

My father squeezes her arm to reassure her. "I'm afraid there's nothing I can tell you." He looks at the rest of the women. "You all know how bad it is. Your men are at their stations doing their duty. They won't leave until their jobs are done. They've got smaller boats in the harbor looking for survivors. The military hospitals and the aid stations are overrun. They're bringing some of the wounded to town. It may take a while for you to get word. You need to be patient."

"Why are *you* here then?" one woman demands.

"My ship is sunk. I'm awaiting orders. I'm heading back now."

He leads us into the hallway to escape the women. "Where's Les?"

"We don't know, Dad."

"Gather your stuff. We're going home."

"Are you sure we should?" Mom asks.

"I want you close by, and we need to find Les."

"Lieutenant Williams, can I ride with you?" Leinani asks. "In case Joe comes home?"

"All right. Mrs. Lowe, we can take you too."

"No, thank you. I'll stay here for now. I feel safer in town. I need to think about the twins." There are tears in her eyes.

When we get in the car, Leinani asks my father to drive her by Aloha Gifts. He tells her he can, but we can't stay long. He needs to get back to base. When we get to the shop, I'm relieved to see that Leinani's parents are fine. It is Sunday, so their shop was closed up tight when the attack started, and they were in their back living rooms safe and sound. And, so far, there is no sign of the Japanese on the beach.

Leinani is grateful to Dad for the ride home. She asks him about Joe, but there is nothing he can tell her that will ease her heart so she sits back in her seat and stares out the window. The roads are still crowded and we are forced to stop at roadblocks along the way. As we finally approach our home, my father explains that martial law has been declared. That means our military is now in charge of the island. There'll be a blackout tonight, he says. We need to keep the lights off or cover the windows so the Japanese can't use our lights to guide their planes.

"Oh sure, let's black out our homes," Leinani says as we approach our housing unit. "Never mind all the fires lighting up the harbor. I'm sure they can't see *that.*"

I'm surprised by how angry she sounds. The day is wearing on her, as it is on all of us. She jumps out of the car almost as soon as it stops and runs into her house, looking for Joe. Something tells me he isn't there.

There's an empty feeling to the neighborhood. My father keeps the car engine running. He opens our front door and shouts for my brother. No answer. "I'm going to tan that boy's hide when he gets home! He won't be able to sit down for a week. What right has he to worry your mother like this?"

"You know Les, Dad," I say, slipping my hand into his. "He always takes care of himself."

"I'm sure you're right," my father says, squeezing my hand.

There's a burst of machine gun fire, and the sky lights up with red tracer bullets. At the sound, I jump.

"I need you to be brave, sailor. Can you do that?"

"I will."

Dad kisses me on the head. He turns to my mother, pulls his revolver out of his belt, and urges her to take it. "If the Japanese come back, use this, Nora. Don't hesitate. Promise me."

Mom nods. Dad draws us both into a hug and climbs into his car. I offer a meek wave as my father backs away slowly with the lights off, and somehow this is worse than when he left this morning. Then, I was too stunned to realize how scared I was. Now, as darkness descends and the fires in the harbor burn an eerie orange and there's the occasional sound of gunfire, I'm more afraid than I've ever been.

6

An Unexpected Visitor

After Dad leaves, we go inside. Mom stares at the gun, then walks to the kitchen and puts it in a drawer. She hates guns. Even when I was little, she wouldn't go with us when Dad took us to shoot cans in a nearby field.

"Come on, Rose. We need to get ready." Mom and I hang blankets over the windows in the kitchen and the living room and put towels under the doors so that each room is completely blacked out. Mom says we'll deal with the other rooms in the morning.

"Fill the bathtub and these two buckets with water," she tells me. She says it's in case a fire starts or the water goes out, but I wonder if she believes the rumors that the Japanese might poison our water supply when they invade.

We take the mattress back to my room, and I remake my bed, smoothing the sheets and pulling my bed back to its place three inches from the wall.

When I was four or five, we lived in a house that had sunflowers along the side of the house. At night, they would cast a round shadow on the wall, like a person's head looking through the window. If I moved my bed a little ways from the wall, only half the shadow showed, which was much less scary. I've kept my bed that way ever since.

I glance around my room to see if anything else is out of order, then come back downstairs. Mom is sitting at the kitchen table, a cold cloth to her forehead, her eyes closed. I know what that means. She has another of her bad headaches.

"I need to go lie down," she says. "Will you wake me the minute Les or your father comes home?"

"Why don't you sleep down here?" I say. "I can make up the davenport for you."

Mom takes both my hands in hers. "I'm afraid it's too hot for my headache. I need to be upstairs where I can open the window. Don't worry, honey. If the Japanese were going to invade, I think they would have done so by now. We're as safe as we can be tonight. But if you get scared, you can come sleep in my room."

She hasn't offered that since I was a little girl and used to get nightmares whenever Dad left to go to sea. Sometimes I would dream a monster was attacking us, and Dad wasn't there to save us. And sometimes I would dream a monster was attacking his ship, and he would never come home. But Mom would tell me if I first said my prayers and then pictured Dad safe on the bow of his ship, he would come home. And he always did.

"I think I'll stay down here for a bit," I say.

"All right. Don't forget to wake me if Les or your father comes home."

I wait for Mom to go upstairs, then check the doors again to see if they're locked and the windows to be sure they're shut. Mom is right—with everything closed up so tight, it's getting really hot in the duplex. At the front window, I ease the blanket aside. I look one way up the street and then the other. All the houses are dark and there is no sign of what Les would call "suspicious movement." But there is no sign of Les either. Why didn't I call out to him this morning and ask where he was going? Then at least we'd know. But he probably wouldn't have told me anyway. Wherever he is, I hope he stays put tonight. There's a curfew, and none of us are supposed to be out until morning.

A streak of tracer bullets lights up the sky, and for

a minute I can see the shadowy figures of destroyed ships and bombed-out buildings. I wonder where on the base my father is. Did he go back to the hospital? Or is he on one of the big ships helping with the rescue efforts? Or on one of the little boats that is skimming along the oily water looking for survivors and picking up the bodies of the dead?

"Please, God, keep him safe," I say, and I close my eyes and picture him standing tall and strong on the pier looking out at the ships. And then I remember the binoculars Dad keeps in the kitchen drawer and run to get them. Why didn't I think of those before! It's silly to hope I might be able to see him, but it's worth a try. It's too dark to focus on much of anything, and the binoculars are not that strong, but when I point them toward the sunken hulk of the *Oklahoma*, I see lots of men standing on the overturned hull. It looks like they are gathering tools and torches and starting to cut through the hull, which means the rumors about men being trapped inside some of the ships must be true. I can't tell if any of the rescuers are Joe, but I'm sure he's there, helping to save his shipmates. Maybe my father is there too. They'll get those men out, I tell myself. They have to.

I let the binoculars dangle from the cord around my neck and replace the curtain. I go and sit down on the davenport. All is quiet on Mrs. Lowe's side of the duplex. She has not yet returned from town. It feels even lonelier knowing there is no one on the other side of the wall. I asked Leinani if she wanted to stay the night with us, but she said she ought to be home in case Joe comes back. I've kept the radio on, but it's mostly silent. Every now and then the announcer comes on with a quick message asking for doctors and nurses to report to a certain hospital or reminding civilians to keep the roads clear and to stay off the telephone.

I can't just sit here in the dark. I need to *do* something. I decide to finish my sketch of the attack. I grab my sketchbook off the coffee table and take it into the kitchen. I turn on the flashlight, and the beam falls across my page at an awkward angle, lighting only part of my sketch. I turn it this way and that until I get it just right. I could turn on the light, but I don't. Even though the windows are covered, and Mom said the Japanese will not invade tonight, I still feel like I'm being watched, like when I was a kid and those sunflowers were bobbing outside my window. If I sit in the dark, though, they won't be able to see me as well.

I close my eyes and try to bring back the images from this morning, but instead, I see a picture of Eddie's face. It's hard to believe that back in California, nothing has changed. My friends are sleeping in their same old beds in their same old houses in same old Burlingame. I wonder if Eddie has heard about the attack yet. If so, I wonder if he's concerned about me and if he'll try to write. If we go to war, will the mail even get through? Will he ever get this sketch? What about the sketches I planned to send him for Christmas? It doesn't matter, I tell myself. No matter what happens, I need to draw what I see.

Deeper into the night, I'm nearly done with the sketch when I hear a light scratching sound on the back porch. I catch my breath. Is it a Japanese soldier's gun scraping against the porch? Did the doorknob just wiggle, or was it my imagination? Still afraid to breathe, I move quietly to the kitchen drawer and remove the revolver. I point it at the door, my hands shaking so badly I probably couldn't hit the side of a barn if I needed to. I let my breath go slowly, but it does nothing to steady my hands. I think about calling for Mom, but I don't want the intruder to hear me and know I'm here. Dad always says the element of surprise is best in battle. He also said to be brave, but that's hard to do when the enemy is right outside.

Just then I hear a muffled whine, and the shuffling again, only this time louder. It's not a human whine, I decide, but I'm not sure what it is. I cross the kitchen on tiptoe and put my ear to the door. There's the sound again, and this time I'm sure. It's a dog!

What if I'm wrong, though? What if it's a trap? Or what if I open the door and the Japanese soldiers see the light from the flashlight and come running?

The dog whimpers louder, and I decide to take a chance. I move the towel that has been blocking the light and open the door quickly, gun to my side. There, near the corner of our porch, squats a medium-sized tawny brown dog with short ears that fold at the top and big brown eyes. He lowers his head and backs farther into the corner, favoring his front paw. Like me, he's trembling all over.

"Come here, boy," I say, scrunching down and patting my leg. But he doesn't budge. I don't want to step outside, but he's giving me no choice. I set the gun down on the porch and present him the back of my hand as I approach him so he can sniff it. He stretches his neck and sniffs my hand. I pat my leg again and try to get him to follow me. He whimpers, but he doesn't move. I slowly sit down beside him, pet him gently, and use my sweetest voice to say, "Attaboy, boy. You're safe now. You're a good boy." He cocks his head and looks at me. I grab his collar and tug at it gently. He pulls back at first, whimpering again, but after a moment he allows me to bring him inside. I tell him again what a good dog he is and keep hold of his collar as I close and lock the door.

At that moment Mom comes into the kitchen, still in the clothes she was wearing earlier. "Rose, what is *that*?"

"It's a dog."

"I can see that. Where did it come from?"

"I don't know. He was outside."

"You shouldn't have opened the door," Mom says, pulling out one of the kitchen chairs and sitting down.

"But he was whining, Mom. I think maybe he's hurt. He's limping a little," I say, pushing his rump down gently so we can look at him.

Mom pets the dog for a minute to gain his trust, then she gently lifts each of his front paws. On his right one, a piece of shrapnel is stuck in the pad. Mom tells me to hold him still. He strains against me at first, but I keep talking to him in my most soothing voice. Mom removes the splinter, and I loosen my grip. The dog scrambles away from me and cowers under the table.

"Does he need a bandage?"

"I don't think so," Mom says. "The wound was tiny and, see, he's standing on the paw now. I think he's fine. What does his tag say, Rose?"

I scoot under the table slowly and gently lift his tag. "Tippy. That's all. Who do you think he belongs to?" I ask. "I haven't seen him around here."

"There's no telling," Mom says with a sigh. "Dogs spook at loud noises. He might have run for miles."

"Can I give him some water?"

"A little. Use the wooden bowl. Don't start getting attached, Rose. This dog will have to go in the morning. We have enough to worry about. I'm sure he'll find his way home when he's ready."

I put some water in a bowl and the dog laps it up, then pushes the empty bowl against the wall with his nose and tips it over. "Silly dog. Guess that's why they call you Tippy," I say. I sit down on the floor, and he comes and lays his head in my lap, the water from his wet chin soaking through my dress. I run my hand reassuringly across his short fur. He's still trembling, but not as much.

My mother goes to the back window and moves the blanket. "I heard you talking. I thought it might be Les." She drops the blanket and sits down at the table, rubbing her temples. I'd forgotten about her headache.

"Do you want me to get you something to eat, Mom?"

"No, we can't be wasting food, Rose. There's no telling when the cargo ships will return from the mainland. I'm sure the Japanese are just looking for ships to sink."

She sounds angry now. And that's how I feel too.

And then I remember I left the gun on the porch. I ask Mom to hold Tippy while I get it. She's not happy I left the gun outside. In fact, I don't think she's happy I touched it at all.

"I don't want you handling this, Rose. A gun is not a toy. You could have hurt someone. You could have hurt the dog." She takes the revolver and puts it back in the drawer.

"I know. I was just scared."

Mom reaches out and I take her hand. She leads

me to the table, and we both sit down. "It's going to be all right," she says, but her voice doesn't sound so sure.

"Mom," I say softly, "why did the Japanese do this?"

"I wish I knew, Rose. Their fight in Asia is not going well, despite having such a powerful military. And they blame us because we've been siding with the Chinese. Or maybe they're angry because we froze their bank accounts in America. Or maybe they just thought they could beat us too."

If Les were here he'd say something brash and heroic. Something like, "Well, they'll be sorry now. Wait till Dad and our navy get their hands on them." But standing here in the dark, with a lost dog in my lap, my mother looking anxious, and still no word from Les or Dad, I don't feel very heroic. I just wish things would go back to the way they were.

The next morning, Mom comes down the stairs. Tippy and I are curled up on the davenport, but when we hear her footsteps, we both sit straight up.

"It's okay," Mom says. "It's just me."

I'm sure the sun is up, but it's still dark in the

living room with all the windows covered. The first thing Mom does is remove the blankets and open the windows. She looks outside for a bit, watching for Dad or Les no doubt. After a moment she sighs and turns away.

The breeze feels good after such a hot, stuffy night. I yawn. Even with Tippy by my side, I didn't sleep well. I woke up with every little sound the house made, thinking it was the Japanese. I reach over and scratch behind Tippy's ear. He jumps to the floor and stretches. Then he goes to the kitchen door and scratches it lightly. It takes me a minute to realize what he wants. I laugh at myself. Anyone should know a dog needs to go outside to relieve himself after a night inside, but this is the first pet I've had to look after. I open the door and stand on the porch while Tippy does his business.

I glance around at the backs of the houses as Tippy sniffs the porch steps. Everything looks normal from this angle, as if nothing has changed. But I can still smell smoke and burning oil, and I can still hear trucks honking as they head toward the base and the occasional loud bang in the harbor, and I remember that the view from my front porch looks far from normal. I sigh and call Tippy inside. When

I come back into the kitchen, Mom is hunched over my sketchbook, which is lying open to my drawing of the attack. She's frowning.

"You don't think it's very good, do you?" I say.

She puts her arm around me. "No, it's perfect. I just wish you hadn't had to see that. I wish this wasn't happening."

As Mom starts the coffee, I get the bread out of the breadbox to make us some toast.

"Turn on the radio," Mom says. "Let's see if there's any news."

The radio takes a minute to warm up, and then I hear the announcer say that President Roosevelt is about to make a speech to Congress. I call Mom in and we sit together on the davenport. Tippy leans against my legs. As the president starts talking, Mom pulls me in close.

Yesterday, December 7, 1941—a date which will live in infamy—the United States of America was suddenly and deliberately attacked by naval and air forces of the Empire of Japan.

The president speaks in a deep, strong, confident voice. He talks slowly, so every one of his words will be understood.

The attack yesterday on the Hawaiian Islands has

caused severe damage to American naval and military forces. I regret to tell you that very many American lives have been lost. In addition, American ships have been reported torpedoed on the high seas between San Francisco and Honolulu . . .

It sounds so strange to hear President Roosevelt say the word Honolulu. So strange to think how far away he is and how alone we are on this island. Just a few weeks ago, Hawaii would have seemed so far away to me too.

Then he says something that gives me hope:

No matter how long it may take us to overcome this premeditated invasion, the American people in their righteous might will win through to absolute victory.

And with that, he asks Congress to declare war on Japan.

Mom and I lean back against the davenport, my head on her shoulder. "Well, that's it," she says. "We're at war."

Tippy lies down across my feet.

7

The War on Our Doorstep

An hour after the president's speech, the war comes
rumbling right up to our front lawn, and I rush to
the window to see. Tippy follows me and puts his
front paws on the windowsill, trying to see out, but
he's too small. I lift him up. Two marines have driven
a truck up our dirt road and stopped right in front
of our duplex. They move around to the back of the
truck and sweep the canvas cover aside. The first
pulls out a machine gun, and the second grabs a
metal ammunition box. The second limps a little as
he follows his buddy.

The first marine starts to set up the gun while the
second returns for more ammunition. Then they dig
in the tripod legs a little to steady the gun. They sight
the gun toward the harbor and then toward the sky,
talking seriously and pointing in different directions.
Then the first marine stands and claps his buddy
on the back. They shake hands, and the first marine

dashes back to the truck and speeds off. The second marine sits down by the gun and stretches out his injured leg. He opens an ammo box and inspects the ammunition belt.

"Mom, there's a soldier outside with a machine gun! What should we do?"

Mom comes to look then turns to me and says calmly, "Take him out a cup of coffee, Rose. Looks like he's going to be there a while."

I grab one of our best cups and fill it with coffee. I walk carefully across the front room, wishing I hadn't filled the cup so full. As I reach for the door I try to hold Tippy back with my leg, but I'm not balanced well and he bolts past me, nearly knocking me over. For a minute I think he's going to run away, and I want to drop the cup and chase after him. But he doesn't. He dashes straight for the marine, who raises his arm to fend him off.

"Tippy, no! Come back, boy," I yell, afraid the marine might hurt him. Tippy does not come back, but he does leave the soldier alone and start sniffing around the yard. I breathe a sigh of relief and approach the marine.

"Now how's about that?" he says, pointing at the cup. "How'd you know I needed a cuppa joe? You're an angel."

I blush. "My mother told me to bring it out," I say, suddenly remembering I haven't combed my hair since yesterday morning and I'm still wearing the wrinkled dress I slept in. "Sorry I spilled a little."

The marine sips his coffee. "You got a name?"

"Rose Williams."

"Hiya, Rose. I'm Private Harold Sanderson. My friends call me Sandy. This here is Sheila." He pats the gun. "She's my best girl. She's gonna keep you and me safe if the enemy comes back, but ya gotta do somethin' for me. Keep your dog inside, okay? I can't have him bumpin' me. This is serious business."

"I will. He's not my dog anyway," I say. "Are you hurt?" I point to his leg.

"Me? Nah. Just twisted my ankle running out of the barracks yesterday morning during the attack. I was trying to get to the storeroom to get one of these babies," he says, patting the gun again. "But I didn't make it that far. Finally just started shooting at the planes with my rifle."

"Did you get one?"

"Nah," he says, screwing up his lip. "They was too far out of range."

"Do you think they'll come back?"

"Hey, now, you aren't scared, are ya?" he asks. "Them Japs are long gone, and if they do come back, they're no match for Sheila and me. Ain't you seen them Japs in the movies? Short and scrawny with them Coke-bottle glasses. We'll lick 'em in no time."

I'm not sure he's right about that. The Japanese pilot I saw didn't look anything like that.

He hands me back the cup. "Tell your ma thanks for the joe."

I take this as my cue to leave and turn around to call for Tippy. He comes running from around the house and bounds up to me. I grab his collar.

As I'm dragging him back toward the house, a car turns onto our street. For a second I hope it's Dad's car, but it's not. There's a woman driving, and when she sees Sandy in the road she slows to a stop. Sandy picks up his rifle and lays it across his lap. The car turns off, and the driver, a middle-aged woman, steps out and says to Sandy, "Can I park here for just a bit? We won't be long." Sandy nods. The woman turns and opens the back door, and out climbs June. She approaches me quickly with her head down and her arms folded in front of her. Sandy watches her closely, both hands still on his gun. I remember what he just said about the Japanese, and I'm so glad June didn't hear it.

June joins me on the porch. "Is your father all right?" she asks, as Tippy licks her legs. She reaches down and, still looking at me, rubs his neck.

"I think so. We saw him yesterday."

"That's good. Is Leinani home, do you know?"

"No, she left this morning to volunteer at the hospital and try to find Joe."

"Rose," Sandy calls. "You might wanna get *that girl* inside. Some folks might not take kindly to a Jap so close to the base."

"Quit calling her that!" I say. "She's not a Jap. She's my friend." I take June by the arm and lead her into the house. She asks about Tippy, and I tell her he's a stray. I lead her into the kitchen, and Mom nods to her quietly.

"Who brought you here, June?" I ask.

"My neighbor, Mrs. Ludens. Her husband is a machinist in town and he came to see if he can help on the base. She dropped him off first. Mrs. Takahashi came too, but when she saw the soldier out front, she decided to stay in the car. She's scared."

"I'll go get her," I offer, but my mother says no, which is odd. It's not like her to be inhospitable.

"Who's Mrs. Takahashi?" my mother says to June.

"My Japanese teacher's wife."

Mother gives a tight-lipped smile. "How can we help you, June?"

"The FBI came for my father last night. They came for Mr. Takahashi, too."

"What do you mean, 'came for them'?" I ask.

"They arrested them. They said they thought my father bought his boat so he could help signal the Japanese during the attack or maybe to smuggle in some of their soldiers. They are arresting any local Japanese they think might be helping the enemy. They came to our house last night and took Papa. They didn't even give him time to grab a toothbrush or a nightshirt. Mama had to run after him with his shoes. We were wondering if Lieutenant Williams could find out where they took him."

"I'm sure Dad can help. Right, Mom?"

My mother stands. She paces the room. "You put us in a difficult situation, June. My husband is an officer in the US Navy. How is it going to look if he's asking after Japanese collaborators?"

"Mother! I don't think her dad is a collaborator. He's just a fisherman."

Mom raises her hand to silence me. "I'm sorry, June, but this is none of our business. If your father has done nothing wrong, I'm sure they will release him soon. I think maybe you should go back to town. Rose, can you please show June out?"

I stare at my mother in disbelief, but she is standing rigid, both hands on the table. There are tears in June's eyes as she rises from the chair. We walk across the front room in silence. On the porch, though, I stop my friend. "I'm so sorry, June."

"I'm scared, Rose. This morning Mama burned everything Oriental in our house, even her wedding *kimono* and her pictures of her parents at their home in Japan. She cried so hard when she tossed those in the burn barrel. She buried my grandfather's *samurai* sword in the backyard, and she said we can't speak Japanese at home anymore, only English."

"That's terrible!"

"Everyone will hate us now."

"But you didn't start this. You're an American."

"Doesn't matter. They'll blame us anyway. Didn't you see the way that soldier looked at me? And you heard your mother."

I cringe at the mention of my mom. "Well, *I* don't blame you. Look, June, I'll ask my dad anyway, even though Mom doesn't want me to. Don't worry, we'll find your father," I say, trying to sound as reassuring as I can.

June reaches into her skirt pocket and takes something out. She glances in Sandy's direction, but he's looking toward the harbor. She grabs my hand and lays a small photograph on my palm. "This is a picture of Papa and the rest of my family. Your Dad can use it to help find my father, if he wants. I wrote our phone number on the back. Tell Lieutenant Williams Papa is not a collaborator. He's just a fisherman who works really hard to take care of his family. He's never broken a law in his life. He's true to America, Rose. I swear it."

I slip my arm around June's waist and walk her to the car. I stand in the road and wave as the car pulls away. This time, I make a wide circle around Sandy, but now that June is gone, he's all smiles again. "Hey, little Rose. You sore at me? Guess that means I can't bother you for a sandwich, huh?"

I ignore him.

"You best watch out," he says, his voice no longer friendly. "Nobody likes a Jap lover."

8

A Promise to Keep

"Quit sulking, Rose," Mom says, as I pick at my tuna sandwich. I'm not sulking, I'm just taking off the bits of crust she didn't cut off all the way. I *am* still upset, though, about how she treated June. I'm about to tell her so when we hear the back doorknob rattle, and though it's the middle of the day and there's been no sign of a Japanese invasion and Sandy is right outside with his machine gun, my heart still stops for a second. I wonder if I'll ever *not* jump at the sound of a doorknob rattling for the rest of my life.

"Nora, it's me."

It's Dad's voice!

Tippy barks and I reach to hold him back as Mom rushes to open the door. There stands Dad. His eyes look tired, but he's smiling. "Look who I found." He steps aside to reveal my brother slouching behind him.

"Les!" Mom and I yell. Mom throws her arms

around my brother, then she holds Tippy so I can hug Les too.

"Easy, ladies," Les says. "Watch the noggin." He points to a fresh bandage wrapped around his forehead.

"What happened!?" Mom asks. "Let me see."

"It's just a bump and a scratch," he says, pushing her hands away. "I'm fine. What's with the dog?"

"Never mind him," Mom says. "Let's worry about you." She pulls Les over to the table and settles him in a chair. "Rose, give him that sandwich," she says, pointing at my plate. I scoot it over in front of Les.

"Tell them everything, son," Dad says, clapping Les on the shoulder. "I need to get out of this filthy uniform."

Les takes a big bite and starts to talk. Mom doesn't scold him for speaking with his mouth full, she just leans across the table and grips his forearm like she's never going to let go.

"So, you know how I went to the dance Friday night? Well, I made a bet with some Chinese kid named Jimmy who lives on a farm over near Aiea. Rose met him. We bet on who would win the Battle of Music that night, and I lost. I rode over there Sunday morning to pay him back.

"I was just planning to give him the money and skedaddle, but I get there and his mom says he's feeding the pigs and I should go on down there, so I do. He's just finishin' up, and we get to talkin,' and then some planes fly over real low, like just above the trees. A few minutes later, all heck breaks loose."

"Les, your language."

"Sorry, Mom. Jimmy tells me to follow him, and we run down to the railroad tracks. On our way there, this Japanese plane takes a few shots at us." He reaches into his pocket and removes a bullet. "See this here? This bullet nearly split me in two, but he missed."

"Oh, Les," Mom says, "give me that nasty thing."

"Not a chance, Mom. I'm keepin' this. It's my good luck charm now." He kisses it and puts it back in his pocket.

"So, after that, we sat on the railroad tracks and we could see the whole harbor. The planes were strafing Ford Island and dropping bombs on the ships, and then the torpedoes hit the *Arizona* and, oh boy, I bet they coulda heard that explosion on the moon! They hit the *Nevada* and the *Utah*, and pretty soon the whole harbor was a burnin' mess. We watched the whole thing. We could even see the planes blastin' Wheeler and Hickam fields, and then we saw our navy shells exploding in the sky. One of those shells downed a Jap plane. Boy did we cheer."

Les asks Mom for a glass of water. I tell her I'll get it. As I'm filling the glass, I look over my shoulder, not wanting to miss a thing. Les takes a big bite of sandwich, and Mom tries again to lift his bandage for a look. He jerks his head away and frowns at her, but it's not his usual playful dodging, it's more a look of warning. In that moment, he looks a bit like Dad when his patience is worn.

I offer Les the water and he takes a long drink. Then he continues. "After a spell, Jimmy's father found us. He brought us back to the house, and his mother had thrown some supplies in their old jalopy. We headed for the hills to hide in one of the caves. It wasn't much of a cave, but his mom felt safer there. Later that afternoon, when it quieted down, his parents wanted to go home and check on their animals, and that's when I got hurt."

"Your head?" I ask.

"Course my head, you ninny. See any other bandages?"

"Les, be kind," Mom says. "What happened?"

"I was running over to get my bike off the porch

so I could ride it home. I tripped over a bomb casing that was sticking part way out of the ground. I fell and hit my head on the bottom step of the porch. Knocked myself out cold."

"Oh, Les."

"Guess they brought me inside the house, and his mom must have patched me up. I don't remember much. Mostly I just slept all night. This morning I was still feeling a bit dizzy, and Jimmy's mom wouldn't let me ride home. She made Jimmy and me stand out on the highway till we could wave down a truck with some MPs headed to the base. I told 'em to bring me home, but they said I ought to have someone look at my head first, so they took me to an aid station on base. They patched me up quick and got me outta there. That's when Dad came by and saw me."

Just then, my father comes down, dressed in a clean uniform. My mother offers him something to eat, but he refuses. "I've got to get back, Nora. They have me working at headquarters now. I'm taking Les with me. We can use some messengers on the base to keep the orders moving."

"But Harlan, Les should rest."

"Look at him, Nora. He's fine."

"Fit as a fiddle," Les says, patting his chest with both fists.

"Don't worry. I'll make sure he's home before curfew," Dad says.

Mom purses her lips but says nothing more.

"Dad, before you go," I say. "My friend June was here. She needs help."

"Who's June?"

"The Japanese girl who went with Rose to the dance," Mom says. "They arrested her father last night. Rose wants you to help, and I told her it wasn't a good idea." She gives me a stern look. "*And* I told her she shouldn't bother you with it."

"Your mother is right, Rose. We don't know who we can trust yet. I want you to stay away from that girl for now, do you hear?"

"But, Dad."

"That's an order."

"Yes, sir." I drop down into my chair, and Tippy puts his head in my lap.

"Now then, what's that dog doing here?" Dad asks.

"He showed up last night," Mom says.

"Well turn him loose."

"But Dad, he can be our guard dog. He can help

keep us safe."

"You're safe enough, Rose. Get rid of him."

I sink down to the floor and wrap my arms around Tippy. A single tear slides down my cheek, but I wipe it away before Dad sees. I thought things would be better if Dad came home. I thought he'd take care of everything. I was wrong.

"Nora, can I have a word with you?" Dad says as he leads Mom by the elbow into the living room.

Les drops down beside me and scoots up close till our shoulders touch.

"Rose, I need you to do somethin' for me," he whispers in one of his goofy voices.

"No."

"Do it and I'll try to convince Dad to let you keep the dog for a while."

"What is it?"

"Go to Jimmy's farm and get my bike."

"But Les, how am I supposed to get all the way to Aiea?"

"You can hoof it. Should only take an hour or two if you hurry."

"I don't really want to go anywhere by myself. Not now."

"You can hitch a ride. Folks are real nice 'bout

givin' rides so long as you're not Japanese."

"Can't you get the bike later? I have something to do." Since Dad and Mom won't help June, I need to find Leinani. I'm sure she'll have an idea.

"No, I can't." Les sounds annoyed now. "I might be workin' till sundown, and then the curfew kicks in." He makes his voice sticky sweet and gives me a nudge. "Come on, squirt, be a sport. I'll owe you one."

"You always say that."

"Yeah, but this time I mean it. Look, Rose, Dad bought me that bike, and you know how he is about us keepin' an eye on our stuff. Besides, I might need it for messengering."

"What am I supposed to tell Mom?"

"Don't tell her anything. She'd never let you go."

"But that would be a lie."

Les looks annoyed. "It's a small lie. This is war, Rose. Do you want to do your part or not?"

I think it over. "Okay, fine," I say quietly. "I'll do it this afternoon. But don't forget to talk to Dad about Tip."

"Good. I hid my bike in the cane field before I left. Jimmy knows where it is." He then tells me exactly how to get to Jimmy's farm. "One more thing."

"What?"

"Take a bag with you. There's plenty of shrapnel around the farm. Spent shells, bullets, pieces of jagged metal, stuff like that. Gather some up if you can."

"What for?"

"Les, time to roll," my father says, coming back in the kitchen.

"I'll tell you later," Les says. "Off to do my duty now." He gives me a sloppy salute.

After he and Dad leave, Mom sits me down. "Your father says they could use another bookkeeper at headquarters. There are so many reports to fill out. He wants me to come over there for a couple of hours. I'm worried about leaving you here, though. Maybe you should come with me."

But if Mom goes, this is my chance to get Les's bike. "No, it's okay, Mom," I say, looking down at the table. "I'm sure Leinani or Mrs. Lowe will be home soon. I'll just work on my sketches until they get here."

"All right then. You can go to Mrs. Lowe's or Leinani's, but otherwise stay put. And if anything happens, run over to headquarters right away. It's the yellow building not far from the gate, remember? I'll be back before dark."

"Can I keep the dog, though? Just for now? For company?"

"I suppose," Mom says. "But he'll have to go by this evening."

Unless Les convinces Dad to let Tippy stay, I think.

While Mom changes into a suit dress, I pull out my sketchbook and add a few more lines to my picture of the attack, but I can't concentrate. All I can do is wonder what's taking Mom so long. Finally, she comes downstairs and pins on her hat. She asks if she looks presentable. I tell her yes, and she gives me a kiss on the cheek and walks out. I pace the kitchen, giving her a five-minute head start, then I grab a small coil of thick rope from the pantry and cut off enough to make a leash for Tippy. I tie a slip knot to one end of the rope and put it over his head. Then I tie a loop at the other end to form a handle and fiddle with it till it fits my hand just right. I can't stand it when things are too tight.

"Okay, Tippy. Let's go."

When I step onto the porch, I see an unexpected sight. Leinani is crossing the yard to her duplex, one arm around Joe's waist, and the other propping up one of his arms. Joe's uniform is torn and bloody, his wavy hair is caked in dirt and oil, and both of his hands are heavily bandaged.

"You found Joe! He's okay!"

"Yes, open the door for us, will you?" she says.

"Of course." I move Tippy out of the way as Leinani helps Joe inside.

"Pull out that chair," she says to me, indicating one of the chairs at their front room table. Leinani helps Joe sit down, and Tippy moves forward to sniff his bandages.

"What happened, Joe?" I ask.

"It's nothing. I'm fine."

"It's not nothing," Leinani says. "He tore up his hands helping in the rescue effort at the *Oklahoma*. They were drilling through the hull to get to the men trapped inside. He grabbed at a piece of jagged metal to keep it from falling in the hole, and he cut up his hands. The doctor says he needs to rest."

"I don't need rest, I just need something to eat. Then I'll go back."

"You'll do no such thing," Leinani says. "You've got to let your hands heal."

"You expect me to sit here while my buddies are trapped?" Joe says. "Ted's in there! We can hear them tapping on the hull. They don't have much time, Leinani. We've got to get them out before the water fills the hull." There are tears in his eyes, and it's the first time I've ever seen a navy man cry.

Leinani steps over and cradles his head to her chest. "They'll get them out, Joe. But you gotta take care of yourself. I can't lose you."

Now Leinani is crying, which makes me want to cry. Tippy goes over to Joe and lays his head on his leg. That dog sure can tell when someone needs a little love.

Joe pushes Leinani gently away and wipes his eyes. Leinani goes to the kitchen. I leave Tip with Joe and follow her. While she makes up a plate of cold cuts, I tell her what happened to June's dad and ask what we should do.

"I don't think there's anything we can do."

"Maybe you can go into town and try to learn something more. Maybe you can figure out where they took him," I say.

"I can't leave Joe. He needs me," she says, cutting up a mango.

I'm shocked. Leinani must not be thinking clearly. "What about June? Doesn't she need you too?"

Leinani slams her knife down on the table. "You don't understand, Rose. You're too young. We're on our own now. All of us. Now go get Joe for me. Tell him his lunch is ready."

Joe is petting Tippy with the back of his bandaged hand, and I let him know what Leinani said about lunch. Then I pick up Tippy's leash and yank him away from Joe. I slam the door when I leave. I had thought Leinani, of all people, would want to help June. She was boasting, after all, about how she'd known June all her life and how much she cared about her. I, on the other hand, have just met June, yet I seem to be the only one who really wants to help. Sometimes I just don't understand grown-ups.

But glancing over toward the harbor, my anger loosens. I think of Joe's friends still trapped beneath the *Oklahoma's* hull, and the sailors who might be trapped on other ships as well. I think about how filthy and ragged both my father and Joe looked in their uniforms and how they've worked through the night to help set things right. Maybe Leinani isn't exactly wrong. Maybe we each have to do what we can right now. Maybe we kids can't leave everything up to the grown-ups anymore. Maybe we have to figure out how to help on our own, scared or not.

One thing I can do is keep my promise to Les. Maybe if he has his bike, he can deliver his messages faster, and maybe one of those messages will have to do with the Japanese who were arrested. Maybe one of those messages will help free June's father. And maybe not. But I have to do something.

"Come on, Tip," I say. "We've got a long ways to go."

9

Jimmy

The buses aren't running yet, so Tippy and I will have to walk to Jimmy's farm. But when we get to the highway, it's still a chaotic mess of cars, trucks, jeeps, and ambulances going to and from Honolulu, and I stop. Can I really do this alone? Can I really go all that way? And where are all these cars headed? Have the Japanese invaded? Are the people running away to town? No, that's silly. Someone would have told me. My imagination is getting away from me. Tippy turns to look up at me as if to ask, "Are we going or not?"

"Be brave, Rose," I say to myself.

As we step onto the highway, I do my best to keep us as far to the side of the road as possible. Even still, several drivers honk at me, which makes me jump. Tippy jerks at his leash, his ears tilting and turning as he takes in all the sounds. I think the noise is making him nervous too. After a mile or so, an old

Ford pulls over in front of me and a woman leans out the driver's side window.

"Rose, is that you? You're liable to get yourself killed in this traffic."

It's Mrs. Barber, our neighbor!

"I need to get to a farm near Aiea. It's important. Something for my mother," I lie.

"Well get in. I'm heading to Pearl City to stay with my sister. I can drop you off."

"Thank you!" Tippy and I crawl in.

"How's your leg, Mrs. Barber?" I ask as we start to drive.

"Hurts like the dickens, but I'll be okay." She gives me a reassuring smile, but her eyes are sad and her voice is softer than usual and I can sense something is wrong. I'm getting really good at recognizing that feeling after the past two days.

"Mrs. Barber, is your husband all right?" I ask quietly.

She grips the steering wheel. "I don't expect he is. He was on the *Arizona* when she went down. She sank so fast, she took most of her crew with her. So, I can't have much hope, can I?"

I don't know what to say. All I can think of is how happy Mr. and Mrs. Barber looked at the dance on Saturday, and how he called me "pretty lady." If Mrs. Barber is right, that most of the sailors on the *Arizona* were killed, then maybe Mrs. Lowe's husband is dead too. I can't bear to think about it.

"I heard someone at the YMCA say some of the men were jumping off the *Arizona* as it was sinking," I say. "Maybe Mr. Barber was one of those."

"That's possible," she says, patting my knee. "I should hope for the best, shouldn't I?"

Her voice breaks, and she bites her lip to keep from crying. I want to tell her she can cry if she wants to, but I'm not sure how to say it. So, I just look out the window and we drive the rest of the way in silence.

We're out in the countryside now, passing rice paddies and swamplands. And then I see the rusty wheelbarrow Les said marks the turnoff to Jimmy's farm.

Mrs. Barber drops me off, and I wave good-bye as she pulls away. Then I walk down the dirt road past the taro patches and a small fish pond covered in water lilies and surrounded by ginger plants. Jimmy's house is very simple and a little rundown. It's long and narrow with a tin roof and a porch running the length of one side. The door is open. I step inside the entryway and call out, but no one answers.

"Try da kitchen," a voice says from behind me. I turn and see a young Chinese man holding his shoes. "It's in da back," he says, pointing with his chin.

Tippy and I walk around the house past the outhouse and toward a shack a little ways down a slope. Inside, there's a small kitchen, and Jimmy's mother is stoking a cooking fire in the wooden fireplace. Jimmy is sitting on an orange crate pulled up to their handmade table.

He stands, and in daylight he looks even younger than he did at the dance. He's wearing too-big overalls with no shirt underneath and he's barefoot, like nearly every kid I've seen in Hawaii, except at school or church, of course. It's not a habit I've picked up yet. I don't like stepping on things that are hot or pokey. I can't even stand it when my socks aren't smooth in my shoes.

"You Les's sista?" Jimmy says.

"Yes. I came to get his bike. He said you'd know where it is."

"Yeah, I know where the bike stay. Us go."

He runs out of the kitchen and waves for me to follow. As soon as we are outside he drops to his knees and pats his chest so Tippy will jump up on him.

"Who dog dat?"

"I don't know. I found him. Guess he's mine for now."

"You got one good *poi* dog," he says, roughhousing with Tip. "How your papa? Les was really worried."

"They sunk his ship, but he's fine. Dad has Les working as a messenger on base. That's why I need the bike."

"It stay hiding. Come, I show you where."

He trots toward the road and Tippy follows him, jumping up on Jimmy's legs and barking. Jimmy just laughs. I try to grab the leash, but Tip is moving around too much. We go past the chicken coop and the pig pens and cross the dirt road again, which runs along the railroad tracks.

On the far side of the road is the sugar cane field Les mentioned. Jimmy tells me about the attack, and his story sounds just like the one Les told. At the edge of the cane field, the grass is high. Jimmy stops and now I can grab Tippy's leash. Tippy's tongue is hanging out. He's panting, but he still clearly wants to play with Jimmy.

"Gosh, he really likes *you*," I say.

"I like him too," Jimmy says, nudging Tip's hindquarters with his bare foot. "Our old dog die. We going get new one after we pay vet bill. Every farm need one good dog."

Jimmy turns and picks up my brother's bike, which I hadn't even noticed lying in the high grass.

"You like supper?" he says.

I think he's asking me to stay for supper so I answer, "No, I need to get home before curfew. But thank you."

As we turn there's a sudden glint of metal in the sunlight, and a loud voice says, "Stop! Don't move!"

An American soldier is standing in the road just behind us, pointing his gun at Jimmy, the bayonet just inches from Jimmy's throat. He yells stop again, and Tippy strains at his leash and barks loudly. Jimmy drops the bike and, with a whimper, raises both of his hands. The soldier is tall and skinny and his blue eyes are narrowed in fear and concentration. His gaze darts back and forth between Jimmy and Tippy, who is still barking madly.

"No shoot, soja," Jimmy pleads. "I just went get dis bike."

"Please don't shoot," I say, my voice shaking. I take one step forward with my hands up.

"Don't move," the soldier says again. His voice is shaking too. I stop.

The soldier looks Jimmy up and down. "You a Jap?"

"No, sir. Me Chinese. Dat my farm." He points very slowly toward his house. "I just went get dis bike," he says again.

"Please," I say. "He's telling the truth. My father is an officer in the navy." Usually people listen to me when I say that, but not this time. The soldier ignores me. His attention is focused solely on Jimmy. Slowly his face relaxes and he lowers his gun.

"You're lucky I didn't shoot you dead. You should know better than to be sneaking around. How was I supposed to know you wasn't a Jap?"

"Me sorry," Jimmy says. He's trembling.

"Stay clear of this road, you two. We're patrolling it now."

"Yes, sir," we say together.

Jimmy picks up Les's bike and we half walk, half run across the road and up the slope toward Jimmy's kitchen. When we are out of sight of the soldier, Jimmy drops the bike again. He bends over and puts his hands on his knees and draws several huge, heavy breaths. I pat his back. It's sticky with sweat. "You okay, Jimmy?"

"No make fun. How you like if some *lolo* soja stick bayonet at you throat?"

"I'm not making fun of you. What was he *doing* there?"

"Dey camp in field down da road. Army. Been there months. We talk with sojas many times. We give 'em food. Dey never give us trouble before."

"I think you just scared him," I say.

"*I* scare *him*! How 'bout *he* scare *me*! Dumb haole. Dey jumpin' at shadows. Dey took my friend Takeo. Yesterday morning. His family Japanese, but dey been on da big fish pond long time. I went see him yesterday morning. MPs came. Dey say to Takeo's parents, 'You got twenty minutes to clear out. We don't want no Japs living so close to the harbor, spying on our ships. If we come back and you're still here, we've gotta take you to the Immigration Station.'"

"The Immigration Station?" I say. "That must be where they took my friend June's father. They arrested him Sunday night. Where is the station?"

"I donno," Jimmy says, picking up Les's bike and starting back up the slope. "Bet my big braddah knows, though. He drive Uncle Dan's taxi sometime.

Make extra dough for our family. He know where everything is."

"Is he home?"

"Yeah, but he going work pretty soon."

"Can you ask him? Please, I need to help my friend."

Jimmy shakes his head at me, but he agrees. We walk the bike back to the front house. Jimmy's brother is sitting on the porch. He's the same young man who sent me to the kitchen earlier. He's polishing his shoes. Jimmy indicates I should stay in the yard, and he skips up the steps to stand in front of his brother.

"Eh, Fred, you know where da Immigration Station stay?"

"Yeah, it's on Ala Moana Boulevard by da piers. Why?" he asks, looking up. At that moment, he spots me in the yard and tilts his head to study me.

"No reason," Jimmy says, backing away.

His brother turns to Jimmy, his shoe in one hand and his polishing cloth in the other. "Eh, Jimmy, I donno what you up to, but if dis about Takeo, let it go. Now not da time to poke around asking questions. We gotta keep our heads low."

"It's not about Takeo," Jimmy says. "Promise."

His brother shrugs and turns his attention back to his shoes.

Jimmy comes back down the stairs and, together, we walk up the road toward the highway. "What you going do?" he asks.

"I don't know. Go to the Immigration Station tomorrow, I guess."

"How you going? It stay all da way downtown."

I look down at the bike. "Guess I'll ride."

"You same like your braddah, one crazy haole," Jimmy says, shaking his head.

"Well, I have to do *something*. June's the only friend I've got here."

"If you want, I show you where it at. My braddah can drop me off in town. Meet me by da King Kamehameha statue."

"Where's that?"

"In front of da palace. He wear one gold cape and helmet and hold one spear. Big statue. Everyone know. Just ask."

"Thank you, Jimmy!"

Jimmy squats down to say good-bye to Tippy. He rubs him hard on both of his sides. Tippy licks his face and Jimmy laughs.

"Hey, Jimmy," I ask. "Did my brother pay you the

money he owes you from the bet?"

"Nah. He was going give me when bombing start. I think he forgot."

"I'll make sure he gets it to you."

"Okay, sure. Or maybe you leave dog here. He no need pay me then," he says with a rascally smile.

I glance down at Tippy, who is sniffing around a shrub by the side of the road, poking at some leaves with his nose. He'd probably love it here, living on a farm with Jimmy, but I'm still hoping Les will talk Dad into letting us keep him.

"Think I'll take him back with me for now," I say to Jimmy.

"Yeah, okay," Jimmy says again. He waves as he takes a few backward steps down the road, then turns and runs toward his house.

I get on the bike and touch my right toes to the dirt, then my left, and then I straighten up and put both feet on the pedals. I always do that before I ride a bike. Not sure why. Guess it makes me feel more balanced.

As Tippy trots along beside me, I suddenly remember Les's other request. He wanted me to bring back shrapnel. I was so concerned with the bike and the soldier that I forgot. As I pedal down the dirt road, I look for spent bullets or bits of shrapnel in the road. I find only a few, small, jagged pieces of metal. I pick them up and put them in my pockets. I still can't imagine what he plans to do with them.

10

A Plan That Cannot Fail

When Tippy and I make it back home, the sun is down and the neighborhood is growing dark. I've been thinking about my plan a lot, and if I'm going to get to town tomorrow without anyone finding out, I'll need Les's bike.

As I'm crossing my yard with the bike, I stick to the shadows near the house, hoping no one will see me. But Sandy calls out, "Curfew, Rose! You keep sneakin' 'round like that, you're liable to get shot." That's no joke, I think, remembering what happened to Jimmy.

"Yeah, I know. Be back quick as a flash."

"Keep that dog inside too."

"I will."

I'm glad to have Sandy and his gun out front, but I sure wish he didn't have to be so loud about everything.

I put the bike on Mrs. Barber's back porch,

leaning it carefully against the house. I double check her door to make sure it's good and locked. Seeing Mrs. Barber's curtains drawn and her windows closed, I feel guilty keeping the bike here when I know why she has left, but I can't think of anything else to do.

I run home through the backyards to avoid Sandy. Tippy goes immediately to the kitchen sink and barks. Smart dog. He's telling me he needs water! I fill the wooden bowl again and set it down on the floor. He laps it up noisily and tips it over again while I scour the kitchen looking for scraps to feed him. For now, I open a tin of Spam and slice off a piece of the meat. I grab Tippy's bowl, put the meat inside, and add a slice of bread. Kind of like a doggie sandwich, I guess. Tippy's so happy, he does this funny jump and twirl as I set his bowl down. He wolfs down the food. If Dad does let me keep Tippy, I'm going to have to find some cans of dog food somewhere. I put the rest of the Spam on a plate and place it in the icebox.

As Tippy gulps down his supper, I run to my room and hide the shrapnel in a hat box in my closet. Then I settle myself at the kitchen table and open my sketchbook to a new page. I pick up my pencil and sketch the outline of the soldier with his gun and bayonet pointed at Jimmy. I draw Jimmy, with his hands raised, and Tippy standing beside him protectively.

After a few minutes, Tippy jumps up and goes to the back door. I hear Les and my mother talking on the porch and quickly close my sketchbook. They can't see the drawing of Jimmy or it will give my whole plan away. Les opens the back door for Mom, who is carrying a half-full bag of groceries. Tippy, in his excitement, manages to get himself tangled up in her legs. She nearly drops the bag.

"Rose, this dog needs to go before your father gets home," Mom says, pushing Tippy away with her foot.

"Dad won't mind, will he, Les?" I look at my brother hopefully, but he stares at the floor.

"What I think Rose means," he says after a minute, "is that Dad would say it's getting too dark to turn him loose now. We wouldn't want him getting in the way of the patrols or running in front of a car during the blackout. They'll never see him driving with their lights dimmed."

I glare at my brother. It's just as I knew it would be. He didn't talk to Dad about Tippy, and he's trying to make up for it now. He nods once at me as if to say, "I did my bit. Now it's your turn."

"Besides, Mom," I say, "he'll just come back. He likes me now. Maybe I should hang up some sketches of him around the neighborhood tomorrow. See if someone claims him."

"That sounds like a real good plan," Les says.

Mom shakes her head at both of us. "Just keep him out from underfoot," she says, opening the ice box to put in a bottle of milk. "The commissary is almost out of food," she says. "We'll need to be careful how we eat. There's no telling when the cargo ships will get through."

She spies the Spam and takes it out. "I can use this," she says. "Rose, fetch me two potatoes and an onion from the pantry. I'll make a hash for supper. Les, you go lie down and rest your head."

Les motions for me to follow him. I get the things Mom wanted and walk into the front room where Les is lying on the davenport.

"Did you get my bike?" he whispers.

"No," I say, looking away. "And *you* didn't talk to Dad about Tippy."

"Don't be a baby, Rose. I need that bike."

"I know, it's just that Joe came home, and he's

hurt, and I was helping Leinani, and then it got too late." I don't like lying, but I confess it's easier to lie to Les than it is to my mother. Especially when I'm angry with him. "I'll get your bike tomorrow."

"You better. I've got important work to do now. I'm delivering paperwork and orders all over the base."

This gets me thinking. "Just the base?"

"What do you mean?"

"I mean, are they going to send you off the base? Like maybe into town?" I ask.

"Yeah, maybe. But that would be a lot easier with my bike. Why're you asking?"

"Just curious. Wish I could be a messenger, that's all."

"Well, you can't," Les says, lying back on the pillow with his arm behind his head. "This is war work. It's not for girls. If I were you, I'd get started on those sketches of that dog. I don't think there's much chance Dad will let you keep him." He shoves me off the couch with his hip. I hate it when he does that.

"Hey, Les, you should give me the money you owe that Jimmy kid."

"Nah. He's probably forgotten about it. Besides, now that the war has started, I probably need it more than he does."

I can't imagine how Les could believe that. He's seen Jimmy's farm. He knows how hard that family has it. I think about how Jimmy was almost killed today just because he *looked* Japanese. What if they make him move away from his home like they did his neighbor? Even though Les doesn't know all that, it's still not right for him to hold back Jimmy's money. I think a bit harder, then say, "But what if he won't give me the bike without the money?"

Les props himself up on one elbow and considers this. He reaches into his front pocket and pulls out a wad of crumpled bills. He stares at them as if he's still trying to decide if he should give me any. "All right, here," he says finally, handing me a dollar. "But if he doesn't ask, bring it back."

As if I would do something like that! I smooth the dollar bill by rubbing it across my thigh, fold it neatly in half, and put it in my skirt pocket. I can't believe it! So far, my plan is working.

The next morning, Tippy wakes me early with a few wet-nosed bumps against my bare arm. I'm back in my room now that Les is sleeping on the davenport again. Tippy tried to jump on my bed last night, but I pushed him down. I made it clear his place was on the rug beside my bed. Usually, I start out sleeping on my right side with my face to the wall, but Tippy would have none of that. He whined until I turned over on my left side and dangled my right arm over the edge of the bed. He butted his head under my hand until I petted him, and then finally licked my fingers a few times and settled down on the rug. I yawn and close my eyes. It's easier to sleep knowing if the Japanese do try to break into our house, Tippy will hear them and bark.

I hold Tippy's collar now as we ease down the stairs. I don't want him waking up Les just yet. I open the back door quietly and wait as Tippy does his business and conducts his usual sniffing around the yard. Then I call him softly back in and fill his water bowl. I sit down to work on my sketch of Jimmy and the soldier. After a while, I hear Mom get up and close the washroom door. I remember I had told her I would hang up some sketches of Tippy today, so I pat my leg to call him over and grab hold of his haunches, trying to get him to sit still so I can see his face. He thinks I'm playing, though, so he stands and turns in circles, snapping playfully at my hands as I try to push him down again.

He stays still long enough for me to do a quick sketch, then gets distracted by a moan from Les and runs to the front room to check it out. He jumps up on the couch and lands on Les's belly. To my surprise, Les doesn't get angry. Instead, he laughs and grabs Tippy in a bear hug. Tippy works to wriggle out of his grasp and then licks his face.

"Les, get that dog off the davenport," Mom says as she comes downstairs. Mom glances down at my rough sketch of Tippy and nods approvingly. She doesn't ask me to help with breakfast, which means she thinks the sketches are more important. I keep working, doing my best to capture all of Tippy's best features, and then write in block letters the words, "Lost Dog. Tippy. Inquire at 501 Fifth Street West."

After breakfast, Mom and Les dress quickly and head over to the base.

I finish my last two sketches of Tippy. Now I have six. As soon as they're done, I do something I would normally never do: I run upstairs and open the drawers of my father's dresser until I find the leather pouch he uses for important papers. I take it to my bedroom, remove the papers carefully, and hide them under my pillow. Tippy cocks his head. "Don't look at me like that," I say. "I know this is wrong, but it's the only way. I'll put everything back the way I found it as soon as we get home." I rush downstairs, Tippy at my heels.

I go to the writing desk and pull out a piece of Dad's US Navy stationery. I drop it quickly, like it's burning my fingers. We've always been under strict orders not to touch my father's things, and I can't help feeling like somehow he will know I took a piece of his stationery. But I have to do this. I'm not sure what a real messenger does, but I'm guessing orders would come on official-looking paper. I have no idea what such orders would say, or whether they'd be written or typed, so I just fold the stationery carefully so the official seal at the top is showing and put it inside the matching envelope. If I show it quickly to the guards, maybe they won't notice there is no writing.

Then I pick up the phone and hold my breath until the operator comes on. She asks me if the phone call is "necessary" and tells me she will be listening. I know what that means. Mom told me the censors have said we can't talk about the weather or what's happening at the base or anything that would tip off the Japanese if they are listening. I almost hang up, I'm so scared. But I have to talk to June.

The phone rings and, luckily, June answers. The operator tells me to go ahead. "Hi, June, it's Rose," I say carefully. "I have that picture you gave me. We should give it to your dad. I know where he is. Can you meet me in an hour at the King Kamehameha statue?"

There is a long pause. Then I hear June say in a measured voice, "That would be very nice. I'll see you there." Someone must have told her about the censors too. I can't hang up fast enough, and I have to put my hand over my heart to calm it down.

I make some sandwiches quick and put those, a thermos of water, and the sketches of Tippy in my mother's beach bag. I get the picture of June's family she gave me after the attack and the dollar that Les owes Jimmy, put them in the leather pouch, and throw that in too. On a whim, I add my sketchbook and pencils. If we see anything important, I want to be able to draw it.

I crack a couple of eggs into Tippy's bowl. I have no idea if that's a good thing to give him, but he gulps them down. He still seems hungry, but I'm afraid to give him more after what Mom said about the food running out. When he's done, I add water to the bowl and then squat down and take Tippy's face in both of my hands.

"Okay, Tip, I've gotta go," I say, slipping the leash over his head and looping the handle around the kitchen table leg. "Sorry, boy, you can't come. It's too far for you to run. You need to stay here. And don't cause any trouble, you hear?" I give him a quick kiss, grab my things, and leave. I hear Tippy barking for me, and I hope he stops that soon! I dash over to Mrs. Barber's house to get the bike and walk it toward the street. Sandy is standing up, staring hard at the harbor. Even now, two days later, some fires are still burning and there's the sound of heavy machinery operating as the men work furiously to get the harbor and airfield back in shape. The harbor looks like a ship graveyard. It hurts my heart to see it.

But Sandy seems to be looking at something nearer than the ships.

"Do you see something?" I ask.

"I thought I saw a body. They say they've been washing up on shore all over the harbor."

My stomach churns as I turn to look. I do see something in the water, but it's far enough away, I can't tell what it is.

"Should I go get someone?"

"Nah, the patrol will be by soon. If it's a body they'll spot him, poor bugger," he says quietly. In that moment he sounds much less confident and looks much younger than he did before.

"How old are you, Sandy?"

"Nineteen. Why?" He's not much older than Les.

"Just wondering."

"Where you off to, Miss Rose?"

"Just hanging some posters of Tippy around the neighborhood. I need to find his owner."

"Well, don't go far," he says, sounding like a bigshot again. "It's still not safe. And stay out of the way."

I want to tell him he doesn't need to talk to me like I'm a little girl, but he probably wouldn't listen, so all I say is, "I won't."

I glance over at Leinani's house and see Joe standing in the window. He too is looking at the harbor, probably at his sunken ship. I wonder if they've rescued his crewmates yet, the ones who were trapped inside. I give him a wave, and he raises one bandaged hand in return. And then I'm off.

Official Business

It takes me an hour to reach Honolulu and find
the King Kamehameha statue. Jimmy is already
there, wearing the same overalls as before, and he's
barefoot, even in town.

"Us go," he says. But I tell him we have to wait for
June.

June arrives very quickly, flushed from running.

"What's happening?" she says.

"I think we might know where your father is."

"We who?"

"Me and him. This is Jimmy."

"Howzit," Jimmy says.

"Jimmy knows my brother. He thinks the
Japanese men they arrested are at the Immigration
Station."

"Come, I show you," Jimmy says.

We walk a few blocks to Ala Moana Boulevard,
and Jimmy points to a pretty cream-colored building

with a sloping tile roof. When we arrive, the big metal doors of the Immigration Station are open and guards are leading out Japanese men in single file. They line them up in rows on the front lawn. There are military trucks with wooden slats along their sides parked nearby. Guards with bayonets stand beside the trucks. Other guards are keeping watch on the prisoners.

"Look like dey taking dem someplace," Jimmy says. "You see your papa?"

June stands on her tiptoes, stretching as high as she can. "I don't see him," she says, her voice urgent.

"Here," Jimmy says, cupping his hands and nodding toward June's foot. June steps into his hands and I drop the bike and grab hold of her waist to steady her. Jimmy lifts her up.

"I see him!" June says. "He's in the second to last row near the end by the pathway." She starts to wave, but thinks better of it. Jimmy lets her down.

"What now?" Jimmy asks.

"I can't go talk to him," June says. "Look at all the guards."

I *do* look at all the guards. I hadn't been expecting so many. What if I get caught? What will they do to me? What will they do to my father? Will my mother ever forgive me if I get either of us in trouble?

But then June starts to cry. And I know what I must do. I screw up my courage and say, "I'll do it. I'll go talk to your dad."

"How?" June asks.

"I have a plan. Stay here." I remove my leather pouch and hand the beach bag to June.

"Wish me luck," I say, as I pick up the bike. I ride across the street with my head high and my back straight, trying to look as "official" as I can. Never mind that my heart is hammering. I approach the nearest guard and wave my leather pouch at him.

"I'm a navy messenger from Pearl," I say. "I have a communication regarding the prisoners." Did that sound formal enough? Did my voice falter at all?

"Let me see," the guard says, eyeing me suspiciously.

It feels like an elephant is sitting on my chest as I slip the paper out of the envelope far enough for the guard to see the navy seal. *This is never going to work,* I think. *He's going to know it's just blank stationery.*

But as the guard is glancing down at it, his officer calls him over. "Look, we're busy out here," the guard says to me. "Take it inside and give it to the guard at the front desk. He'll look it over."

He turns away and the elephant steps off of my chest. I glance over my shoulder. June is standing with both hands clasped in front of her mouth, her eyes wide. Jimmy, though, is grinning and waving me on.

I nod at him and push Les's bike carefully up the walkway past the rows of Japanese men who are standing with their heads down. At the end of the second to last row, I pause. Still looking ahead, my fingers gripping the handlebars, I whisper to the man next to me, "Pass this to Mr. Nakamura." I hold out the picture of June and her family.

The man doesn't move. I say it again, but he pretends not to hear me. He looks as nervous as I feel. The man next to him, though, reaches out. I give him the picture and watch as he passes it to Mr. Nakamura, who is standing beside him. June's father takes the picture. His hand flies to his stomach and his breath draws in. He glances in my direction. I smile.

"Where are you going?" I whisper.

The man who first took the picture whispers back, "Sand Island, we think."

Then the guard calls to me.

"Hey, girl. What're you doing?"

"Nothing," I say. I move my bike toward the front doors and look back. The guard is still watching me, so I go inside. There's another guard sitting at a desk, but he's talking to someone so I stick close to the wall, count to fifteen, and then head back outside, hoping that seemed long enough. As I'm leaving, though, the guard from outside appears before me, blocking my path. He lays a hand on my shoulder, still looking at me with distrust.

"Did you give him the message?" he says, indicating the guard at the desk.

"Sure did. Gotta get back to base now."

I brush past him and hop on my bike, riding as fast as I can down the walkway. Guards yell, "Hey," as they jump out of my way. I fly past Jimmy and June without looking at them, in case the guards are watching. At the next intersection, I stop and lean over the handlebars to catch my breath. I feel sick to my stomach but also pretty excited. I pull the bike onto the grass beside a large tree with fruit dangling from it that looks like wooden sausages hanging on ropelike stalks. It's the strangest looking tree I've ever seen. I wait for Jimmy and June to catch up.

"Did you give him the picture? Did you talk to

him? Did you tell him I was here?" June says in a rush.

"Kind of. I talked to the man next to him. But your dad saw me. And he got the picture."

"Where are they taking them?"

"Sand Island, wherever that is."

"Dat way," Jimmy says, pointing toward the harbor. "No more road, though. No bikes. You gotta take a boat. Dat good, though. Not far. Maybe dey let you visit your papa soon."

June sits down in the shade of the tree and starts to cry again. Jimmy and I sit on either side of her. I put my arm around her. "It's going to be okay, June," I say. "I'm sure they won't keep him long. He didn't do anything wrong, remember?"

"That doesn't matter. They've taken more of the men we know, including our Buddhist priest and our next-door neighbor who just sells insurance. Mrs. Takahashi wants to get a lawyer, but my mother is too scared. We all are. What if they take us too?"

"No way," Jimmy says. "Too many Japanese here. Where dey going put everybody? Sand Island too small."

"I'm sure Jimmy's right," I say. Although really, I have no idea. This place is still new to me. These people are new. And things are happening so fast. Just a couple of days ago, June and I were sitting on the beach watching the surfers. Now, my father is serving in an actual war, June's father is arrested, and Jimmy can't even walk around his own farm without having a gun pointed at him. And I have no idea how things are back home for Eddie or Esther or my grandparents. We have no way to reach them to find out. Will the war spread to the mainland too? Will anything ever be normal again?

"I know what we need to do," I say, tearing open the beach bag and taking out my sketchbook and pencils. "We need to draw a picture of what we just saw."

"What good will that do?" June says.

"I don't know, it just helps."

"How?"

I'm already drawing as fast as I can. "You know. When you draw something, it's not just inside you anymore. It's out, and all your feelings come out with it. And when you can't explain something to someone because maybe they've never seen it before, like this crazy tree, or maybe they can't imagine it or maybe they don't believe you, it's right there on the page. And they can see it. And they have to believe it. And you can look at it and remember everything. This way, we'll never forget."

June gets up and turns her back, and I wonder if I should stop. But Jimmy points to my sketch of the Immigration Station and tells me to make it bigger. He corrects some of my details on the trucks as I draw those. We decide to put June's father in the front row, so everyone can see him better. That's when June turns back to watch. When I sketch her father's face, she says, "Give me the pencil." She erases what I drew. "His face is longer, not so round. Like this," she says. She takes her time getting his eyes and ears and nose right. Jimmy and I just watch.

We stay by that odd-looking sausage tree for half an hour and finish our sketch. Then it's time for June to get home. She says her mother almost wouldn't let her come. She wants June to stay close to home now. Even if they open our school again, June says her mother may not let her come back.

"Then I'll come and see you," I say.

June doesn't answer. She just gives me a big hug and walks off.

I ask Jimmy if he wants a sandwich and he takes it gladly.

"What're you going to do now?" I ask Jimmy.

"I go fool around, you know? I hear dey putting barbed wire all over da beaches to keep da Japanese out. I like see dat. My braddah going pick me up later. You like stay?" he says.

"I've got to get home and hang these sketches around my neighborhood. I need to find Tippy's owner."

"Okay, den."

"Oh wait, I almost forgot." I pull the leather pouch out of the beach bag and take out the dollar. "Here's the money Les owed you."

Jimmy's face spreads into a wide grin. "I never think I was going see dis dough." He kisses the money and shoves it in his pocket.

"What're you going to do with it?" I ask.

"Donno. Give it to Mama, I guess . . . *after* I go buy some shave ice." He waves and runs off, his bare feet slapping the sidewalk.

I hop on my bike and touch one toe to the ground then the other, like I always do, and start the long ride home.

12

Tippy

On my way home from town, I stop and hang the posters about Tippy near the highway and around my neighborhood. I ask the guards if I can hang the last one near the main gate of the base, figuring more people will see it there. But one of the guards tells me to go away. "Don't you know there's a war on?" he says. "People have better things to do than worry about some dumb dog."

"Tippy's not a dumb dog," I insist. "He's someone's pet. And I'm sure they're missing him, especially now."

"The kid's right," the other guard says. "You can hang it across the street, on that light post."

When I get back to our duplex I hear Tippy barking inside, louder than he did when I left. He sounds upset. I unlock the back door quickly, but when I do, Tippy dashes by me. I try to reach for him, but he's too fast. He's tearing across the neighbors' yards, trailing his leash. I drop Mom's beach bag on the porch and run after him, calling his name. But he's long gone.

I sprint back to the house to grab the bike so I can follow him, but when I pass our open door, I happen to look inside. It's a mess! In his fear at being left alone, Tippy has destroyed our kitchen. He's knocked over the table and shredded the newspaper. There's a puddle beneath his overturned water dish and another where he peed on the floor. The throw rug by the sink is in tatters. He even managed to open a cupboard and a bag of rice has spilled everywhere. There are scratch marks on the door.

When Mom sees this, I'm done for! And now I'm not sure what to do. Do I clean up this mess before she sees it or go after Tippy? I have to at least try to find him. This is all my fault.

I push the bike around to the front of the house.

"Sandy," I call, "have you seen my dog? Did you see which way he went?"

"Nope, but good riddance, I say. He's been raising a ruckus all morning."

I notice Joe sitting in a lawn chair in front of his duplex, his hands still bandaged, a far-off look on his face. I dash over to him.

"Joe, have you seen my dog?"

Joe looks up, and it's like he's never seen me before.

"Your what?"

"My dog. The one you were petting the other day. Did you see which way he went?"

He just gives me that far-away look.

I pedal furiously around the neighborhood, calling for Tippy, but there's no sign of him. I go around two more times and then out by the highway, hoping he didn't get hit by a car. Still nothing. I jump off the bike and walk it home. It's impossible to ride when your eyes are clouded with tears. The closer I get to our duplex, though, the more hope I feel. Maybe he came back while I was out. Maybe he just needed to run off his energy after being trapped inside. I hurry home, but the only thing that greets me is the mess.

I glance at the clock. Mom and Les will be home soon for supper. I grab a rag and soak up first the water, then the pee, crying all the while.

The back door opens. "What happened?!" Mom exclaims.

"Tippy did it," I say, holding out my hands to stop her from coming closer. "I left him alone and he got

139

upset. Don't be angry, Mom. I'll clean it up."

"Why did you leave him alone?" she says, slamming her handbag down on the table. "What on earth is going on here?"

Without thinking, I tell her everything. How I rode into town to help June and how we saw her dad and how I hung up the posters when I got home and how I looked all over for Tippy, but he's gone, and I can't find him anywhere.

"You've had my bike since yesterday? You told me you didn't get it," Les says, looking as angry as Mom now.

"Where was the bike?" Mom asks. So, I tell her all about that too. Might as well, I'm already likely to be grounded for a month.

"You've been up to a fair amount of mischief, young lady," Mom says, sighing heavily.

"I know, but I had to do something. Les said I could help the war effort if I got his bike. And none of the rest of you would help June, so it was up to me. And I hate this stupid war. Why did it have to start? Why are so many bad things happening? Why did they take June's dad, and why did Mr. Barber have to die, and what if Dad dies too?" I'm sobbing now, my whole body shaking. "I want things to go back to the way they were. I wouldn't complain anymore about Hawaii. I wouldn't ask to go back to California. I wouldn't even ask if I could keep Tippy, if I just knew he was safe. I don't want something to happen to him too."

Mom crosses the floor swiftly and pulls me into a big hug. Les puts a hand on my shoulder for a second and then, to my surprise, reaches for the rag to finish cleaning up the mess. Mom ushers me into the front room and sits me down on the davenport. She doesn't say anything at first. She just smooths my hair while I cry. Then she takes me by the arms and sits me up straight. "That's enough now," she says gently.

I nod and wipe the tears from my face.

Mom sighs. "I'm sorry, Rose. I've been so worried and scared, I didn't see how much you needed us."

"You're scared?" I ask.

"Of course. We all are."

"I'm trying to be brave, Mom, like Dad always tells us to be. I thought it was pretty brave to go out to Jimmy's, even though the Japanese might have been hiding anywhere along the way. And I felt awfully bold when I walked past those guards today. But now Tippy's gone, and I don't want to be brave anymore. I just want all of this to stop!"

"Oh, darling, we all want that," Mom says, her voice cracking. "But that's not going to happen. Everything's going to change now, and we have to change with it. We're going to have to keep being brave and strong until this war is over. It's the only way we're going to win. It's the only way we can help your father and Joe and everyone else who has to fight this terrible war. But *I* need you to be brave, Rose. I can't do this by myself."

That's the first time my always capable mother has ever said she can't do something alone. In all our moves, in all the times my dad has been away, in all the times Les has gotten into trouble, my mother has never asked anyone for help. Certainly not me.

"How about we be brave together," Mom says, patting my knee.

"No need, ladies," Les says, strutting into the front room like a cowboy in a Western. "*I'm* here to protect you."

Mom rolls her eyes. "Well, that certainly makes *me* feel better. How 'bout you, Rose?"

"Oh yeah. Much better."

"Hey, now," Les says, arranging his face into a fake pout.

"Come with me, John Wayne," Mom says,

heading for the kitchen. "Let's get you fed."

"I'm thinking steak for dinner, Ma," he says. "I'm a workin' man now. I've got a big appetite."

"You'll get Spam and eggs."

"Again!"

I walk over to the window and look once more for Tippy, but something tells me he's not coming back. Mom's right, things are going to be different now. The sunken ships in the harbor remind me of that.

Outside, Sandy, still manning his machine gun, stands and stretches his back. He looks my direction, catches sight of me in the window and holds his hand low to the ground, a quizzical look on his face. He's asking if I found Tippy. I shake my head. He spreads his hands in a "what-can-you-do" gesture, and I nod. He gives me a thumbs-up and turns back toward the road.

13

Remember Pearl Harbor

Christmas has come and gone. There were no presents this year. Everyone has been too busy to shop, and the supply ships haven't been able to get through from the mainland anyway. The shelves are pretty bare. We did each get oranges, candy, and bubble gum in our stockings, though. And Mom promised to buy us something special when we get back to California, but I told her she didn't need to. Not for me anyway. I wasn't being noble, it's just that all I really wanted was to spend Christmas together as a family—Dad, Mom, me, and Les—and we did.

Mom made a roasted chicken, buttermilk biscuits, and a pineapple upside down cake, because pineapple is one thing that is *not* hard to find in Hawaii! There was no Christmas tree. The ship carrying those didn't make it through either. But I made a tree out of cardboard pieces that I glued together and painted green. I cut out circles of paper from my sketchbook and decorated them like ornaments. I hung those and a string of red tinsel on the tree. We set it on the coffee table. Les made fun of it, mostly because it wobbled, but after dinner we all gathered round it and sang Christmas carols. Even Les. Mom said it was the Christmas tree she would always remember. Dad said he couldn't have done better himself.

But Christmas Day, like every day since the attack, wasn't all smiles. Mrs. Lowe left that day with her twins. Since her husband had died and her babies were so little, the navy had prioritized her to head home to the mainland. Mrs. Barber went too. As it turned out, she hadn't gotten all of the shrapnel out of her leg after all and would probably need a surgery to remove it. She seemed better when she arrived at our house to say good-bye and to help Mrs. Lowe get to the ship, but she said she figured she should head home to Connecticut to live with her parents until her leg was fully mended.

Mrs. Lowe let me hold both of the babies while she borrowed a piece of paper from Mom to write a note to the Japanese girl who had been her housekeeper and nanny before the attack. She had not seen the girl since that awful Sunday three weeks ago.

"I guess she's too embarrassed or afraid to come back," Mrs. Lowe said. "But if you see her, can you give her this? I just wanted to wish her well."

Mom took the note and said, "Of course." As I handed the babies back, I gave each a kiss on the head. We've said good-bye to many neighbors and friends every time we've moved, and I've always felt sad for myself, knowing how much I'd miss them. This time, I felt sad for Mrs. Lowe and Mrs. Barber, knowing they would never see their husbands again.

Most days we do our best to adjust to this new world. Dad is waiting to be reassigned to a new ship. Mom is still helping at the headquarters. Les is still working as a messenger. I've taken over Mom's chores around the house. I'm doing most of the cooking and cleaning now.

Tonight is New Year's Eve. We've invited Joe and Leinani over this evening to celebrate. We'll play Monopoly and listen to the radio and sing "Auld Lang Syne" at midnight, like we always do. And I'll try to pretend like 1942 will be as good as any other year, even though I know that's not true.

Any day now, Mom, Les, and I will receive our orders to evacuate home. The military wants all nonessential personnel to leave the islands. Mom tried to argue they needed her at headquarters. She wanted to stay near Dad. But Dad convinced her he'd be shipping out soon, and he'd worry about us less if we were on the mainland.

So, we're going back to California, back to Burlingame. I wrote to Eddie and Esther to tell them, but the way things have been going, I might arrive home before my letters do. It will be strange to see them after all that has happened. The whole world knows about Pearl Harbor now. It's famous. And I'm sure my friends will have so many questions. This time, maybe all of them will want to see my sketches. But right now, I'm more concerned about getting home. I'm nervous about being out on the ocean. It will take at least ten days for us to reach California, and the Japanese subs could sink our boat. Dad says the captain will zigzag the ship to make us harder to hit, and we should be fine, but that doesn't make me feel much better. I'm not the best swimmer, and I don't intend to take any chances if we wind up in that cold, dark water. I'm going to wear my life jacket at all times.

We'll only get 24 hours' notice before our orders come to evacuate, so we've packed all our belongings already. There are boxes everywhere. We're living out of our suitcases for now. Dad went into town this morning to sell our car. Les took off on his bike. He didn't say where he was going, but I think I know. He's been selling the shrapnel he's been collecting to the tourists at the hotels who will be shipping out soon too. They want it for a souvenir. He hasn't told Mom or Dad. I'm sure they would not approve. I guess some things haven't changed.

Mom is cleaning the kitchen, and I'm sitting on the davenport making a copy of the sketch I did the day we went to the Immigration Station. I've decided to give the original to June, but I want to keep a copy for myself too. I don't think either of us ever wants to forget that day.

As I'm copying that crazy sausage tree, there's a knock. "I'll get it," I say.

And through the door I hear it. A bark. A familiar bark! I fling the door open and there stands a young woman in a navy-blue dress, holding a leash. At the end of the leash is a dog. A dog who jumps up and puts his paws on my thighs, his tail wagging so wildly his whole rear end shakes.

"Tippy!" I drop to my knees and give him an enormous hug.

The woman holds out one of my posters, the ones I hung up weeks ago and never got around to taking down. "I saw this poster a few days ago and I've been meaning to come by," the woman says. She glances past me to the front room full of boxes and says, "Is this a bad time?"

"No. It's a great time."

"For heaven's sake, Rose," my mom says, coming up behind me. "Invite our guest in. I'm Nora Williams," Mom says, as she clears some boxes off the davenport. "This is Rose."

"I'm Violet," the woman says as Tippy jumps up on the couch and circles twice before plopping down. Mom frowns, and Violet pulls at his leash. "Tippy, get down. Bad boy."

"He's fine," I say, helping him off the davenport. "Thanks for bringing him back. Where did you find him?"

"Oh, goodness," Violet says, sitting down next to me. "He's mine, you see. My husband got him as a pup before we were even married. Tippy came home a couple of weeks ago, but I only just noticed your poster near the main gate."

"Oh," I say.

"My husband, Howard, was stationed at Hickam

Field. We were in our apartment the morning of the attack, and Tippy was tied up outside by his doghouse. We ran downstairs after the bombs started falling, and Howard told me to head to town. Howard tried to grab Tippy, but Tippy was too upset. We couldn't get him into the car, so my husband let him run off. We figured he'd come home, but he didn't. Not for days."

I feel guilty then. He never came home because he was with me.

"Well, I bet your husband was glad to get his dog back," Mom says.

Violet does that funny thing women do when they're trying not to cry . . . she sucks in her breath, raises her chin, and looks at the ceiling.

"Actually, Howard was killed manning a machine gun during the attack," she says in a soft voice.

Now I feel even worse that Tippy had not been with her to give her comfort when she found out about her husband. Tippy's good at that.

"I'm so sorry," Mom says. She pauses for a moment, out of respect for Howard. "Is there anything we can do?"

"Well, there might be something," Violet says with a sniff. "I was hoping you could keep Tippy.

See, with Howard gone, I'm heading back to Illinois. I'll try to get my old teaching job back, and I'll be too busy to tend to Tippy."

I look expectantly at my mother, the words *please, please, please* running through my mind.

"I'm afraid we can't, Violet. We're evacuating too."

I slide off the davenport and pull Tippy into my lap, burying my face in his neck.

Violet looks at us both. "I understand . . . I don't know what to do with him. I sure wish I could find him a good home. I hate to just turn him loose when I leave. I know Howard wouldn't want that. There's no telling what would happen to him."

I jump to my feet. "I know of a place. The perfect place."

"Where, Rose?" Mom says.

"Jimmy's farm near Aiea. Jimmy and Tippy get on like a house afire. Jimmy's old dog died and his family needs a new one, and Tippy would have plenty of room to run and play."

"That sounds wonderful," Violet says. "But I'm not sure how to get him there. I don't own a car."

"I can take him," I offer. "I'll see if Leinani can drive me."

"I don't know, Rose."

"Please, Mom?"

"All right," Mom says, finally. "I guess you can leave him here, Violet."

"Oh, thank you," Violet says, hugging first Mom and then me. "Can you tell Jimmy I appreciate this? Tell him Tippy's a good dog. And he's smart. He can even do a few tricks. Watch this." She asks Tippy to "shake," and he holds up his paw. She tells him to "lie down," and he does. She commands him to "say hello," and he barks. And I wonder why I didn't think to see if he knew any tricks.

"This is the best one, though," Violet says. "Tippy, salute." Tippy raises and lowers his paw in a quick and sideways salute, and we all laugh.

"Oh, and give Jimmy this." Violet reaches into her purse and takes out two twenty dollar bills. "This will help pay for his food and care. I wish I could do more." I feel nervous holding onto that much money. It's probably close to a month's earnings for Violet. I fold it in half carefully and push it deep into my pocket.

Violet squats down and tells Tippy to shake again, but this time she holds onto his paw and kisses it. "Have you noticed how his paws smell like popcorn, Rose? Isn't that the oddest thing?" She turns back to Tippy. "You're a silly dog, Tip, but I love you. Be good for Jimmy. Don't forget us, though. Don't forget Howard. Not ever."

She stifles a sob again as she stands, and Mom puts an arm around her shoulder. "Don't you fret. He'll be fine."

Violet turns to me and holds out the poster. "I suppose you'd like this back."

"No, you should keep it. So you don't forget either."

That night, after the party, Tippy sleeps in my room one last time. I tell him to stay on his rug, but after a lone firecracker goes off outside, he starts to whine. "All right, come on up," I say. "But don't tell Mom."

Tippy jumps up on the bed and plops down beside me. I drape my arm around him and feel his chest rising and falling. He turns once to lick my face, then settles down for the night. We lie there together, and I think about everything that has happened. Tomorrow, I will draw this scene, me and Tippy together one last time. That's how *I* will remember him.

The next day, I walk Tippy over to Joe and Leinani's. Joe answers the door. Only one of his hands is bandaged now, but the other one is covered in peeling scabs and nasty pink scars. Leinani is packing too. Joe will be fit for active duty again soon, and, like my Dad, he'll most likely be shipping out. So Leinani is moving back to town to live with her parents and help with the store. When I ask if I can get a ride to Jimmy's farm, Leinani hesitates. "I'd love to help, Rose, but there's so much to do here."

"Ah, come on, Lei," Joe says. "The drive will do us good."

As if to help convince her, Tippy sits at her feet, looks up, and relaxes his jaw into his best doggy grin.

"You win," Leinani says. "I'll get the keys."

"Can we go and get June first?" I ask. "There's something I want to give her, and I think she'd like to see Jimmy again. He helped us find her father."

Leinani agrees. She calls June's mother to let her know we're on our way. June is waiting on her *lanai* when we arrive. She runs down the walkway toting the gas mask we're all required to carry now. It's as big as a leg of lamb and just as heavy. Tippy is sitting on top of mine. I push him and the gas mask to the floor of the backseat as June climbs in. Tippy jumps right into her lap, though he knows better. I tell him to get down, but June says she doesn't mind. She rolls down her window more so Tippy can stick his nose out as Leinani drives.

"How's your dad, June?"

"We haven't seen him, but they've already let some of the fishermen go. One of them came by to see us a few days ago and said my father is fine. He thinks he'll be released soon."

"And your teacher?"

"It's not looking so good. He wasn't just a teacher at the Japanese school. He was also a leader in our community. They say that makes him more dangerous. Mrs. Takahashi is very upset."

"I'm sorry, June . . . If your dad comes home, do you think your mom will let you go back to school after all?"

"I don't know. There's no talk of them opening the schools anytime soon. Maybe by the time they do, she won't be so nervous anymore."

At Jimmy's farm, we find him and his mother again in their little kitchen and wish them Happy New Year. Then I explain why we've come. When I mention them keeping Tippy, Jimmy looks to his mother for approval. She nods, and Jimmy whoops.

He grabs Tippy's front paws and dances him around. I give Jimmy the money Violet left, and he hands it to his mother. Jimmy asks if we'd like to see the farm, and Joe says yes. Joe reminds us he was a city kid, and says he's never been on a farm before. While we're watching the pigs root around in the dirt and mud, he laughs. "They're so big," he says. It's the first time I've heard him laugh since the attack. Leinani notices too. She gives me a smile and loops her arm through Joe's. Then they start to get all soppy, so June, Jimmy, and I look away.

Before we drop June off at her home, I give her the drawing of the day at the Immigration Station.

"Thank you. I'll never forget that day. And I'll never forget you, Rose," June says.

"Do me a favor," I say. "When your father returns, make me a new sketch and send it to me in California. My address is on the back of my sketch."

"You have my word," June says. She gives me a huge hug and tells Joe and Leinani she'll see them soon. She stops on her lanai and turns to give me a wave, holding the sketch to her heart.

As we drive home in silence, my gaze turns toward the harbor. When I was a little girl in church, I figured out if I strained my eyes a certain way while looking at the flame on the candles, I could blur my vision. I do that now, and for a minute the harbor looks as perfect as it did that Saturday morning I first tried to sketch it – all of the ships upright, their flags flying, the sailors standing at attention on their decks. It's a beautiful sight. But when I relax my eyes, the real harbor comes into view, where the sunken *Arizona* is now a tomb to Mr. Barber and Mr. Lowe, and the overturned *Oklahoma* reminds us of the lucky sailors, like Ted and Larry, who were saved by brave men like Joe, but also of the thousands of others who died that day.

Already, though, the harbor is coming back to life. The *Pennsylvania* sailed for America for repairs, the *Maryland* is seaworthy again and so is the *Tennessee*. They say the *Helena* will be back in action and maybe some of the other ships too. My father says they might even be able to salvage his ship, the *Oglala*. And they'll build more ships, big and powerful, and my father will stand bravely on one of their decks with his eyes to the horizon.

They say if you throw your lei over the side of the ship, and it drifts back to land, you will one day return to the islands. I asked Leinani's mother to make a lei I can give to my father when we leave. I'll tell him to be sure he tosses it overboard, so I know he will arrive safely back to this land someday. And when the war is over, he'll come safely home to us!

As for me, I'll make a lei out of paper flowers and drop it into the water, so that someday I can see Leinani and Joe and June again and maybe even Jimmy and Tippy. And in the meantime, when we get back to California, I won't put up the pictures of movie stars over my bed anymore. I'll hang the sketches of my friends and of this beautiful place that was home for such a short time. That's how I will remember.

Meet the Real Rose Williams and Jimmy Hu

Peggy Baccelli and Jimmy Lee

Sometimes the most interesting people you could hope to meet live right in your own hometown. They might be your neighbors or friends or just people you stand in line with at a grocery store. That's one thing I love about studying history. Fascinating stories are all around us, we just have to seek them out.

Margaret Jane Littmann Baccelli is known as Peggy to her family and friends, and she lives just across town from me. On the day I first met Peggy, she showed me a painting her father had made of the Japanese attack on Pearl Harbor as seen from their front yard. That painting was often in my mind as I wrote the battle scenes in my book, and you can see it on my website.

Peggy was thirteen years old and in the eighth grade when her family moved to Pearl Harbor, Hawaii. Like Rose's father, Peggy's dad was a communications officer on the USS *Oglala* and her mother was a capable navy mother, managing all the family moves. In real life, Peggy had three older brothers, not just one. Her brothers Don and Bob served in the navy during the war. Bob's plane was shot down, and he was killed in action.

When Peggy and her father, mother, and brother Vince arrived at Pearl Harbor, they were awaiting housing of their own, so they lived with her aunt and uncle and their son and twin baby girls. Her uncle was also in the navy. In my story, the aunt became Rose's neighbor, Mrs. Lowe.

Peggy was a shy girl and doesn't recall making any good friends in the short time she lived in Hawaii, but she does recall two Japanese girls in her class who would leave after school to go to Japanese school. That memory inspired me to include the character of June in my book.

Peggy did not tell me about the "Battle of Music" and the dance in which the ten-year-old girl won the jitterbug contest, but those things really happened! I found them in my research. Peggy did, though, enjoy watching the boxing matches at Bloch Arena with her brother. She and Vince also collected matchboxes with ships on the covers. She referred to

Vince as "kind of a wandering kid, just curious about things," and that description helped me to create the character of Les.

Peggy really did watch the attack on Pearl Harbor from her front yard, and it happened much as I describe it in the book. Her dad did run to assist at the base during the attack and later tried to help at the hospital. And Peggy and her mother, aunt, brother, and cousins were evacuated to the YMCA in town, where Peggy's father later found them.

Many of the little details in the book come from Peggy's memories, including her brother making small dishes (which I referred to as ashtrays) out of coconut shells and how Peggy had to craft her own Christmas tree. But I also wanted to explore the treatment of the Japanese and Japanese Americans in the days immediately after Pearl Harbor, so I added in that storyline. You can read more about Japanese internment during the war in my book, *The No-No Boys*.

But even though Peggy's memories provided me with lots of great material, I still felt the book was missing something. Then, on a research trip to Pearl Harbor, I was told of a wonderful man who volunteers his time at the Pearl Harbor Visitor

Center and speaks to thousands of schoolchildren from around the world. His name is James "Jimmy" Lee, and like the Jimmy in my book, he grew up on a farm near Aiea on the shores of Pearl Harbor. Jimmy's farm looked much the way I describe it. And though he never met or helped a navy officer's daughter named Rose, he *did* have a soldier point a gun and bayonet at his throat!

Jimmy was eleven years old in December of 1941. He was the sixth child in his family and had lots of chores on the farm, including milking the cows, feeding the pigs, and tending to the vegetable patch. On the morning of December 7, Jimmy had gone out to feed the pigs when the Japanese began their attack. He sat on the railroad tracks and watched the bombs fall. "We were not afraid at first," he said. "We thought it was a war game, and I ran to see the show." His memories of watching the attack are the basis of the story Les tells in *War on a Sunday Morning*, with some additions on my part.

As in my story, Jimmy and his family did seek shelter toward the mountains in the Waimalu Valley. When he returned home, Jimmy realized his best friend and neighbor, Toshi Yamamoto, had disappeared. The Jimmy in my book shares a similar story. In real life, Jimmy did not find out until seventy-one years later what really happened to Toshi, and how he and his family were forced to leave their home because they were Japanese.

A few days after the attack, Jimmy had gone to get the family cow, which had been tied up in the cane field. There was a curfew on and it was still dark. A soldier appeared out of nowhere and pointed his gun and bayonet at Jimmy. Though Jimmy was Chinese, the soldier had mistaken him for a Japanese invader. That was a story too good not to appear in my book!

So, what happened to my two Pearl Harbor kids when they grew up? Well, Peggy worked for a while as a clerk for the Southern Pacific Railroad and then married Albert Baccelli. They had three daughters. She later worked as a pre-school teacher, and Peggy is an artist, just like Rose!

When Jimmy grew up, he joined the Hawaii Air National Guard and was later drafted into the army. He went on to serve in the U.S. Army Corps of Engineers and eventually retired after forty-two years of federal service. He enjoys traveling and spending time with his ever-growing family.

And what about Tippy? Tippy is made up,

although many survivors of the attack on Pearl Harbor remember how much the noise and confusion affected their pets. Many dogs did run away or hide or even get injured. Tippy gets his name from my husband Roger's family. Roger grew up on a farm, and all of his dogs were named Tippy, just as all of his father's dogs had been. When I asked my father-in-law why all the dogs were named Tippy, he said it was partly because they had painted the name Tip on the doghouse, so the name just stuck.

To see pictures of Peggy and Jimmy and learn more about the real Home-Front Heroes, visit my website at **www.teresafunke.com**. And take a closer look at the cover of this book. The illustration is meant to look like Peggy.

If You'd Been Friends with Rose Williams or Jimmy Hu

If you'd been friends with Rose Williams or Jimmy Hu, you might have:

Mourned the LOSSES AT PEARL HARBOR. Though many people, especially those associated with the military, knew the Japanese might attack America, they were not sure where. Many did not believe it would be Pearl Harbor. And most people were caught completely by surprise when it happened on that Sunday morning in December 1941. In the attack, 2,403 people died. Most were military personnel, but 68 were civilians, including several children. Another 1,143 people were injured. Twenty-one US Navy vessels were sunk or damaged, including eight battleships, like the ones Rose was drawing at the start of my book. In addition, 188 aircraft were destroyed and 159 were damaged. Those are the planes Violet's husband would have been fighting to protect. Not a single person on the island was unmoved by the horrible losses of life and property, especially those closest to the base, like Rose, who saw the carnage up close. Everyone feared an enemy invasion of the island that, fortunately, never came. Though most residents of Hawaii felt sadness, fear, anger, and confusion after the attack, they also felt hope, strength, compassion, and determination. One thing was certain, none of them would ever be the same.

Lived under MARTIAL LAW. As you saw in my book, martial law was declared within hours of the attack on Pearl Harbor. This meant the military assumed control over the islands. Martial law was partly put in place to deal with what had previously been labeled the "Japanese problem." People of Japanese descent made up 37 percent of the population of Hawaii, and there was fear they would help the enemy, which is why June's father was arrested (remember, you can read more about Japanese internment in my book, *The No-No Boys*). So, after the attack, the army commander, General Walter Short, was put in charge of life in Hawaii. Almost immediately, a curfew and a blackout were ordered. People covered their windows with tarpaper, heavy curtains, or paint. Censorship of the press, long-distance phone calls, and the mail was instituted. The army closed the schools until February. And all civilians, even children older than six, were fingerprinted and required to carry identification cards at all times. Soon, everyone was told to use a special US currency stamped with the word "Hawaii." Barbed wire, sandbags, camouflage, trenches, and armed soldiers were everywhere. Life had changed overnight for the children of Hawaii.

Carried a GAS MASK *and* BUILT A BOMB SHELTER. Every citizen of Hawaii, including the children, was issued a gas mask, to be carried with them at all times. This was to protect you in case the Japanese did invade the island and release a poison gas. Even babies were issued "bunny masks," which were large breathing bags into which you would place the child. They were decorated with bunny ears to make them appear less scary. Children often had to don their masks and participate in drills in which they sought cover in trenches or public bomb shelters. Speaking of bomb shelters, your family might have built one in your own backyard. The locals called them "scare pukas." Personal bomb shelters were often little more than holes in the ground, covered by wood and topped with dirt. Many filled with water after a rain, and one woman told me they also filled with bugs, frogs, and mosquitoes.

DONE YOUR PART. "Remember Pearl Harbor"

became a battle cry for our country. Kids all over the United States answered President Roosevelt's call to aid in the war effort. They participated in rationing, war bond drives, and scrap metal and rubber collections. They also tended to "victory gardens." You can read more about those activities in my other Home-Front Heroes books. The children of Hawaii also did their part. Boy Scout and Girl Scout troops stepped up to help the police, the military, and the hospital workers. Many children also got one day a week off of school to help in the pineapple fields. Some kids volunteered in hospitals and evacuation centers. Others helped in stores and businesses when the men joined up to fight and watched the little kids while the women and remaining men worked. How would you have liked to help the war effort?

Glossary

Ahi – yellowfin or big-eye tuna

Aku – skipjack tuna

Aloha – Hawaiian word used for greetings or farewells

Braddah – Hawaiian Pidgin for brother

Caucasian – English word for white people or those of European descent

Commissary – a store that sells groceries and supplies on a military base

E komo mai – welcome/come in

Haole – a person who is not native Hawaiian, most specifically a white person

Jap – a common but unkind word during World War II to describe people of Japanese ancestry

Kimono – a traditional Japanese garment worn for important occasions

Lanai – an open-sided porch or veranda

Lei – Hawaiian garland made most often of flowers, leaves, or shells and worn around the neck or head

Lolo – crazy or stupid

MP – an abbreviation for military police officer

Malihini – a newcomer or visitor to Hawaii

Oriental – of, relating to, or coming from eastern Asia

Pau – finished or done

Pidgin – a grammatically simplified form of a primary language, like English

Poi dog – a mixed-breed dog, named after an extinct breed of dog on the islands

Puka – hole

Sampan – a Japanese fishing boat used in Hawaii

Samurai sword – a sword belonging to a Japanese warrior of the upper class

Sista – Hawaiian Pidgin for sister

Soja – Hawaiian Pidgin for soldier

Strafe – to attack repeatedly with mostly machine-gun fire from low-flying aircraft

Taro – a plant with an edible root similar to a potato

Acknowledgments

People ask me all the time which of my books is my favorite. I tell them it's impossible for me to answer. I love all my books, just like I love all my children. And because all of my novels are based on real people, they are each special in their own way. Each of my books, though, has taught me something new and provided me with a unique challenge. *War on a Sunday Morning* taught me to keep going, even when I felt stuck or unsure, which I often did. If I didn't give up on the book, it wouldn't give up on me. This story wanted to be told, and it wouldn't let me set it aside. It forced me to make tough choices, even about things like the cover and title. But those were not choices I wanted to make alone. Thank you to all the schoolchildren, teachers, librarians, writers, book buyers, and friends whom I polled to help me make those decisions!

War on a Sunday Morning required a great deal of research, including reading dozens of books and personal accounts and taking a research trip to Pearl Harbor. I also talked to several people to help me understand life in the territory of Hawaii during World War II, military life, the cultures of Hawaii, the pidgin language, and the details and aftermath of the attack. Primarily, I relied on the memories of Peggy Littmann Baccelli, who was the inspiration for my character Rose, and Jimmy Lee, who was the inspiration for my character Jimmy Hu. You can read about them in the "Meet the Real Home-Front Heroes" section of this book.

I also interviewed Dorinda Makanaonalani Nicholson and gained great knowledge from her wonderful nonfiction book, *Pearl Harbor Child: A Child's View of Pearl Harbor from Attack to Peace*. My cousin's wife, Michelle Meierotto, and her mother, Candy Luis, and aunt, Gail Matthews, also shared with me their experiences of growing up on Oahu. And I'm grateful to Kay Koike and Betty Berry, two Japanese American sisters who grew up on Oahu and shared their memories with me. These very generous people also reviewed my book after it was written and offered input to make the story more accurate.

I could not have completed this book without the help of several very knowledgeable people who took the time to meet with me in Hawaii, show me around the base and the island, offer assistance with research, and in some cases, review my manuscript.

They include the following: Scott Pawlowski, Chief of Cultural and Natural Resources, WWII Valor in the Pacific National Monument; Stan Melman, Assistant to the Curator, WWII Valor in the Pacific National Monument; Johanna Fuller-Yeomans, Cultural Resource Specialist, WWII Valor in the Pacific National Monument; Dr. John Rosa, Department of History, University of Hawai'i at Manoa; Lisa Ontai, Vice President of Marketing and Mission Advancement, YMCA of Honolulu; Marcia Kemble, Manager, Tokioka Heritage Resource Center, Japanese Cultural Center of Hawai'i; Natalie Tuiletufuga, Assistant Buyer, Pacific Historic Parks. If I forgot anyone, please know you have my thanks.

At one point, when I was wondering why I was struggling so much with this story, I realized it was because when I wrote all my other books, my children were young and could offer input and edits as I wrote. What I was missing this time to make a great book was the kind of insight only careful young readers can provide. So, I want to thank my middle-grade reader-editors, Renee Easterbrook, Bran Schneider, and Naomi Sherman, for providing comments and suggestions on my final draft that made this book so much better! And thanks to Delainey Shafer, who also read the final draft and gave it her seal of approval.

I'm grateful to the members of Slow Sand Writers Society, who hung in there with me as I painstakingly pieced this story together: Jeana Burton, Sara Hoffman, Leslie Patterson, Elisa Sherman, Melinda Swenson, Debby Thompson, and especially Karla Oceanak. Special thanks to my friend Laura Resau, who reviewed the book with her son Bran, and to my friends Laura Backes, Karye Cattrell, Pat Stoltey, Gary Raham, Jim Davidson, Linda Osmundson, and especially Natasha Wing, who offered their support, encouragement, and advice.

It was glorious to once again be working with my awesome design team: Kendra Spanjer, who patiently went back and forth with me until we had the cover illustration just right; Launie Parry, whose cover design really pops; Erin Rogers, who has done an amazing job on the interior layout of all my books; and Veronica Yager of YellowStudios, who creates my e-book editions.

Special thanks to Jennifer Top, my copy editor extraordinaire. And, of course, to my assistant, Katie Huey, who contributes so much to my books and business.

Though my kids are grown up now, they still wanted to help. My youngest daughter Ava read an early draft of the book and offered great suggestions, especially about Rose. My daughter Lydia read the final draft to me *out loud* so I could hear my mistakes and offered her very best input. My son Brian helped transcribe some of my interviews. All three of my children are ready and eager to help whenever I need them, but it was Lydia who kept prodding me to "get back to my writing" this time around.

And of course, my biggest thanks go, as always, to my husband Roger. On our daily walks, he listens patiently as I talk through the challenges of writing, publishing, and selling books. During one of those walks, when I was complaining about feeling stuck, he suggested I add a dog to the story. What a great suggestion that turned out to be!

And finally, thank you to all of my fans, supporters, colleagues, and friends who encourage me to keep capturing memories of wartime America in my books. They remind me often that those who don't study and learn from the mistakes of our past are doomed to repeat them.

About the Author

Teresa R. Funke writes for children and adults. Most of her books and short stories are based on real people and actual events, and many are set in World War II. *War on a Sunday Morning* is the fifth book in her Home-Front Heroes collection. "Ask anyone who was old enough to remember where they were when they heard about Pearl Harbor, and they can tell you. Even seventy-five years later!" Teresa says. "It's a memory that will be with them always. So, it seemed impossible to write a series about wartime America and not include the incident that brought us into the conflict. I wanted to put my readers in the middle of the action by setting my story in Hawaii, so they could see what it would've been like to live through one of the most important events in our nation's history."

Teresa also enjoys teaching new writers as a

popular presenter and writers' coach. You can watch free writing videos on her website or her YouTube channel. Teresa loves to read, travel, and go to movies and live theater. What she likes best, though, is spending time with her husband and three children at their home in Colorado. She'd love it if you would visit her website at **www.teresafunke.com** to submit your own family's stories from World War II or other time periods, or to invite Teresa to speak at your school in person or via video conference.

Coming Soon From Teresa R. Funke

A New Home-Front Hero

Summer 1944

Just outside the town of Greeley, Colorado, there's a camp. A big one. It houses 3,000 German and Italian prisoners of war (POWs). They are soldiers, captured on the battlefields of Europe.

On a nearby farm lives twelve-year-old Charlie and his family. When they are told the POWs will be brought to the farms to help bring in the harvest, they become suspicious. What good will it do to have enemy soldiers working their fields? Surely trouble will follow.

"Don't ever believe a prisoner of war likes you. He doesn't," Charlie is warned. But is that true? Read along to discover how an unlikely friendship forms between a farm boy with a special challenge and a German soldier far from home.